Arkansas Breakc

John Harvey is a prolific writer of westerns and thrillers; he also w children's fiction and poetry and edits and publishes a magazine of writing and photography called *Slow Dancer*. At present he is doing research and a little teaching in the American Studies department of Nottingham University. He likes watching movies and one or two other things.

In the same series

Hart One: Cherokee Outlet
Hart Two: Blood Trail
Hart Three: Tago
Hart Four: The Silver Lie
Hart Five: Blood on the Border
Hart Six: Ride the Wide Country

John B. Harvey

Hart Seven: Arkansas Breakout

Pan Original
Pan Books London and Sydney

Okay, Angus, this one's for you

First published 1982 by Pan Books Ltd,
Cavaye Place, London SW10 9PG

ISBN 0 330 26640 3
Photoset by Parker Typesetting, Leicester
Printed and bound in Great Britain by
Collins, Glasgow

One

Tap Loughlin eased himself away from the wall, his throat dry, tongue moving across lips that were cracked and filmed with sweat and dust. The dust was fine and near white and as Loughlin chipped at the stonework around the iron bar, more of it sprayed over his lean face, whitening the dark lank hair unkempt on his head. His eyebrows and lashes were finely coated, his skin felt as if it had been rolled in powder. He shifted his balance a little, his left arm in danger of going numb as it took most of his weight. The bunk swayed perceptibly beneath him and springs creaked. Loughlin angled his right arm so that he could insert the broken knife blade into the growing space above the bar. His knuckles hit the wall and the implement was jarred between his fingers. Grasping at it, he caught nothing. A swift intake of breath and then the clatter of the knife against the stone floor.

'What the hell!'

The voice hissed angrily from the opposite side of the cell and Lloyd Majors swung underneath his end of the bar and stared at Loughlin hard.

'Shut it!'

Loughlin glared back at Majors and held out a hand before him, fingers spread, signalling Majors to wait and listen. There were guard's footsteps off in the distance, not coming nearer but moving away. Somewhere, an inmate was whistling, a hymn tune that both men recognized but neither could have named. Their church going had stopped early. Closer, a prisoner coughed with a harsh, retching croak that continued for minutes without relief.

Nobody had heard the knife drop.

Lloyd Majors turned back to his work and continued to prise the end of the bar loose from the stone into which it had been set. Loughlin climbed quietly down from the upper bunk at his side of the cell and retrieved the blade. They were confined in a space barely big enough for two double bunks, two buckets, a single enamel bowl. Nothing more, no table, no chairs. If the two men got off their bunks at the same time, they had to squeeze past one another sideways to move. Twice a day a guard would bring trays of food which would be slid under the double-barred cell door – dark, watery stew in which the only meat would be scraps of gristle, hard, flat bread, oatmeal, water. That was their diet. Once a day they were allowed out for exercise: a walk round an enclosed compound under the eyes of three armed men with orders to shoot them down if they deviated from the path already worn into the ground.

Not only Majors and Loughlin, but a number of other prisoners as well. It varied between eight and a dozen, depending upon how many had been hanged at the previous dawn. These were the special category cases, hardened and dangerous criminals whose lives were already forfeit and with whom no risks could be taken. The State Penitentiary had a proud record of not losing a condemned man until the hemp had done its work; the governor had no intention of blemishing that achievement.

Once inside the cells the chances of escape were fewer still. Apart from the double bars on the doors, there was a window too small for a man to squeeze his head through and this was heavily barred too. Over the tops of the line of special category cells there ran a thick wire mesh, attached to four thick lengths of iron running through the stone walls. Above that was a gap of four feet and then the roof, stout timbers covered with tarpaulin. Watching over the roof and the compound close by, a guard sat in a twenty-foot tower with a searchlight, a siren and a Winchester.

Tap Loughlin didn't want to hang. Neither did Majors. It was about the only thing they agreed on then, or were ever likely to. The time they had been thrust into that small stinking cell together was the first time they had met. Now they shared each other's nightmares and the stench of one another's bodies. Loughlin had run a small gang of outlaws and like-minded gentry since late in the 1870s. They made a speciality of skipping across the Arkansas and Missouri borders, stopping a stage here, robbing a small bank there, always keeping a few paces ahead of the law and never over-reaching themselves by being too greedy. Once in a while, they'd ride over into Indian Territory, but usually found the competition there a little hot. Everything had been going fine until Tap met up with Sara-Lee Danziger, a Springfield schoolteacher with large blue eyes, a neat figure and an almost overwhelming passion for the works of an English writer named William Shakespeare. When she tired of getting Tap to recite to her Romeo's speeches from *Romeo and Juliet*, she persuaded him that what he really ought to be doing was holding up a train. Not just any old train, but the special which carried gold bullion and bank notes down from St Louis to Texas. Tap Loughlin had thought it a fool idea and had half a mind to tell her so, but she'd fixed him with her blue eyes and he knew he wasn't going to get out of it so easy. Besides, it would be a sight better than reciting Shakespeare.

So Loughlin had done the thing properly; he'd ridden the track in both directions, noted the best places to stop a train, where to hide horses, where to blow the caboose, everything. He and his men had gone through the plan so many times, it seemed impossible that anything could go wrong. If the railroad company hadn't been experimenting with plainclothes detectives among the passengers that trip, it all might have passed off fine. As it was, before Loughlin and the survivors of his gang got away with most of the gold and money, there were five dead men scattered up and down the train, to say nothing of another six wounded, two of them women; one more man took a fatal bullet in the back as he jumped on to his horse, another was shot through the side of the head after he'd galloped maybe thirty yards. Of the total of seven killed, three were working for the Atchison, Topeka and Santa Fe Railroad Company, the other four had been riding with Loughlin.

One of the wounded men was a farmer returning home with a brand new mechanical hoe in the freight car, one was the driver of the train – the others were Tap Loughlin and his right-hand gun, Baptiste LaRue. Loughlin took a flesh wound from a .44 and suffered mild concussion after being hit around the head several times with a long-handled coal shovel. LaRue was shot twice in the right leg, on both occasions missing the bone, and hacked through the left hand with a single-bladed knife which one irate passenger attacked him with when he was trying to crawl away into the scrub alongside the track.

The rout didn't end there. Two days later, the butt end of Loughlin's gang ran smack into a sheriff's posse at a place called Garfield, north of Beaver Lake. They were less than an hour's ride from the Missouri border. Two more were shot and killed, two captured and brought back to join Loughlin and LaRue in Fort Smith prison to await trial.

What the sheriff's posse didn't recover was the haul from the train – which meant that there were still two of the gang at large and those two had between them somewhere around six thousand dollars. Loughlin had never had time to count it.

The thought of all that money somewhere out there, a good share of it belonging to him, was yet another incentive for Tap Loughlin to get out of prison. To say nothing of what Sara-Lee and himself would do with it when it was retrieved.

She'd been there in the public section of the courtroom when Judge Isaac C. Parker had lived up to his name as the 'hanging judge' and sentenced Tap to be swung from the neck until dead for his part in organizing and leading the attack on the train. Baptiste LaRue and the two others, Little Kinney and Scott Levy, were let off with twenty years' hard labour apiece.

Lloyd Majors was sentenced to death on the same day but his case was of a different nature altogether. A heavy-set, glowering man who spent the first eighteen years of his life in and around the dockyard slums of New York City, he came west with a wagon train and spent the following ten or so years acting as a guide and wagonmaster for various groups of settlers heading out across the Great Plains towards the far west. Majors drank a lot and gambled almost as much. When he had liquor enough inside him he was emblazoned by a lust that could only be slaked by one or more whores who'd grown accustomed to taking a little beating with their work and were capable of shrugging their shoulders and putting it on the bill.

One particular time, stopping off in Fort Smith, Majors had got the call without money in his pockets to pay for a visit to the whorehouse, it all having been spent on whisky and lost at poker. He was wandering through the warren of small streets and alleyways that fed off the main square when he came upon Lewis and Katherine Grant, brother and sister and the pair of them a few years short of eighteen.

When Lewis attempted to prevent Majors from forcing his attentions upon his sister, he was punched in the mouth and kicked a few times for his pains. Getting up a minute or two later and hearing Katherine's screams, seeing her clothing torn and hoisted up about her body, Lewis jumped on Majors' broad back. He was thrown brusquely off and hurled back against the nearest wall. When he slumped forward, arms spread, Majors lunged a slim, sharp knife between his ribs. Lewis died, choking on his own blood, gripping the immovable shaft of the knife, hearing his sister's screams for help.

Tap Loughlin had listened to the evidence in court and watched Lloyd Majors' unmoved, unmoving face. He had taken as rich a dislike to the man as it was possible. Forced to share a cell with him, Loughlin had complained to the guards, to the governor. Finally, unable to do anything about it, he had simply ignored the man as much as he could in such a confined space. It had only become impossible to ignore him altogether when he conceived his plan of escape. He needed Majors to assist him and, in return for his freedom, Majors agreed.

Loughlin settled again on the bunk and, with extra caution, raised the knife to the wall. He peered over his shoulder at the heavy form of Majors across the cell; once they were outside the penitentiary he'd make sure that the two of them headed in different directions and never met up again. The thought of what Majors had done made Loughlin's skin crawl. He even thought it wrong and a sinful shame that the other man was about to escape the gallows. Hanging was the only thing for a mad dog like Lloyd Majors – unless it was shooting him down like a dog.

'What the hell you starin' at?' Majors snarled.

'Nothin'.'

'Then get on with that damned wall.'

'I am!'

Majors snorted. 'Huh! Why I let you talk me into this, I don't know. A dumb-ass scheme figured out by a cheap outlaw who couldn't even stick up a train!'

Loughlin's fingers tightened around the end of the blade. His eyes narrowed and he thought about all the satisfaction he would get from driving the jagged point into Majors' bulging, cord-like neck.

Majors read the truth in Loughlin's face and laughed.

'You wouldn't have the balls!' he jeered.

'What for?'

'For usin' that.' Majors nodded at the knife in Loughlin's hand.

'Don't you be too sure.'

'Don't waste your breath threat'nin' me. First move you make towards me, I'll take that toy away from you and break your head open on this stone floor. Tell the guards I caught you breakin' your way out and put a stop to it.' Majors laughed at the thought. 'Shouldn't be surprised if they didn't give me a reprieve.'

He shifted his body across the narrow bunk.

'Maybe I should do that anyway. Get myself free and a parole into the bargain.'

Loughlin shook his head. 'Don't bet on it, Majors. You'd have to get this knife off me first. I ain't some young kid who don't know what he's doin'. Wouldn't be so easy finishin' me. You'd best stick to kids and girls if you know what's good for you!'

Lloyd Majors sat up on the bed, swinging his legs round more quickly than Loughlin had seen him move before. His eyes seemed to be pressing out of their sockets and the length of sharpened metal he had in his right hand was tapping down into the opposite palm.

There was no doubt that he was seriously considering embedding it into the top of Loughlin's head.

Tap for Tap.

Loughlin held himself tense, ready to spring down. If it did come to a brawl, he knew he'd have his work cut out, the other man a good twenty or more pounds heavier. He would have to make the blade count first time, or he'd have little chance. Loughlin watched Majors' face carefully, but the anger slowly subsided and the fingers round the metal began to loosen.

'Outside,' Majors said softly, tapping the metal once more, 'that's where we'll settle this. Outside.'

A pause and then Loughlin shrugged: 'Suit yourself. Just let's make sure we get there.'

Majors brought the sharpened length of iron down once more and closed his fingers around it, squeezing hard. When he lifted the metal away, the imprint of his hand was clear about its edges. With a quick leering smile he turned on the mattress and went back to his task. Loughlin waited a few more moments, fighting down the impulse to leap across there and plunge the blade into the back of the man's neck.

Instead he turned himself and shifted back into position. Soon the only sound in the cell, apart from the breathing of the two men, was the slight scraping and chipping as the ends of the long bars were freed to the point where a good hard yank would take them out. That would be the beginning. For the rest to work depended upon other people than themselves.

Baptiste and Little Kinney swung their picks in time, over their shoulders and then down into the rock-hard earth, breaking up the sods into smaller chunks which could be turned by the hand-drawn plough. They were chained together at the legs, another dozen men on either side of them, swinging and picking, swinging and picking.

Back of them a guard stood with the brim of his hat pulled low to keep the sun out of his eyes; he had a stubby cigar clamped into the corner of his mouth and a shotgun cradled across his chest, resting on his arms. Every move of the work team, every swing of the pick axes, he watched keenly, looking for the first deviation, the first sign of laziness or insubordination – even of escape. A couple of days after Loughlin's two former gang members had been added to this particular work detail, one of the prisoners had made his bid for freedom. Complaining of stomach cramps, he had got himself freed from the long linking chain and had gone off into the bushes to relieve himself. Two other prisoners, bribed beforehand, had started a fight to distract the guard's attention. The man in the bushes had taken off towards the river.

It was his misfortune that the posse of prison guards that set out after him was much slower than the dogs. By the time the guards had arrived, guided by the frenzied barking and the dying screams, the escaper had been torn to pieces.

The couple who had begun the fight were forced to stand up to one another, bare fisted, and punch each other until both were at a bloody standstill. Once they had recovered, they were chained to a fence before all of the other inmates of the penitentiary and whipped close to their lives.

Neither Baptiste nor Little Kinney had any illusions about what would happen to them if their scheme went wrong. But the odds – set against twenty-five years of hewing and digging as well as their share of six thousand dollars – seemed small indeed.

They knew that attempting to escape from field work was the obvious thing to do, in that you were already beyond the prison walls, but it was also the quickest to be detected. The baying of the hounds each night made the disadvantages of being caught only too clear. The plan Tap had devised, and which he had got to them through one of the trustees he'd managed to bribe, was more complicated but – if it worked – safer. It depended a great deal upon the third member of the outfit, Scott Levy, whose leg wound had got him assigned to inside duties until it healed up. A little dextrous work with a piece of stick had made sure that the wound stayed bad enough to keep him where he was most useful. Levy worked in the kitchens, occasionally in the hut that was laughingly called the prison hospital. It was through him that the knife blade and length of iron being used in the cell had been obtained. It was also Levy who had slipped to Tap Loughlin the extra food and tobacco with which the guard had been bribed. More than that, it was Levy who would get hold of the guns.

Not on his own.

There were two others involved in the breakout.

Gideon and Joseph were black brothers; at one time it's possible they had another name but neither of them knew what it was; it was also possible that their dates of birth were logged somewhere, but neither brother knew where. Gideon always claimed that he was the eldest and Joseph likewise. What was beyond doubt was that each was four inches over six feet and a number of pounds in excess of two hundred. It was this great physical strength and an apparent willingness to work which had singled them out to work on one of the governor's special projects. His wife had decided that the two-acre strip of rough land beside their house would be more useful and pleasant if it were transformed into a garden, so Gideon and Joseph had been detailed to clear the land, level it, dig it and – under the woman's guidance – plant small trees and shrubs, flowers and vegetables.

This they did with one guard overseeing them: a procedure the brothers had got used to when working on a cotton farm down deep into Mississippi. One which they had endured until the plantation owner had taken it into his head to make an example of one of them and have him publicly whipped. Since the offence was making indecent advances at his youngest daughter, and since both brothers knew full well that it had been the daughter who had been advancing at the time, they naturally objected.

In the resulting fracas, three of the owner's white overseers were badly injured, one of them having his head stoved in with the end of a piece of picket fence. The plantation owner's eldest son tried to make use of a double-barrelled shotgun and had the stock broken across his back for his pains – the back itself was broken in the process. Gideon and Joseph eluded the pursuing dogs and the police force of Bogalusa, escaping north up the Pearl River as far as Jackson. They robbed a store for food and clothes and the takings from the cash box, did the same in Yazoo City and went across the state line into Arkansas. Here they kept themselves going by a mixture of labouring work and petty crime until one night they ran foul of a US deputy marshal and wound up in the State Penitentiary close by Danville on the Petit Jean.

The man guarding the two blacks usually leaned back against the house wall with a shotgun resting on the ground beside his right leg. He had a Colt .44 holstered on the same side, the gun belt high on the hip and a safety thong over the hammer.

All the work in and around the penitentiary ceased at sundown. That was the rule. The governor's wife, however, was anxious to get her garden finished before her relations came over from Little Rock to stay a while. On this account, Gideon and Joseph were kept working for an extra couple of hours, using the light from a kerosene lantern to wield their pick and shovel. After this time, they were taken in and fed separately in the kitchen. By Levy.

It had taken Scott Levy some time to get the confidence of the two blacks, who weren't too sure that they were any better off outside the prison than they were inside it. But eventually the promise of being able to ride with Tap Loughlin's gang – and get a percentage of the railroad money – convinced them.

'This goes wrong,' Gideon had said to Levy, 'we're goin' to have a pack of hounds chewin' on our ass!'

'Yeah,' added Joseph, 'an' that's just for starters!'

'Don't worry,' Levy had gulped, turning away with a slight but obvious limp, 'everything's goin' to be all right.'

But there was strain in his eyes and sweat on his forehead as he said it.

Two

Gideon's arms moved through a slow but powerful arc, taking the shovel up into the air and then driving it down at a slanting angle into the earth; as it neared the ground his leg moved with it and the underside of his boot met with the upper edge of the blade. The shovel was forced deep into the ground, Gideon leaned his weight against the handle and then lifted the blade clear. A load of earth and stones was hoisted high and then thrown in the direction of a growing heap off to the left.

Meanwhile, Joseph was squatting close to the lantern, using a short-handled hammer to break up large pieces of rock that had been dug out earlier. These would later be carted off and used as foundations for a new wing of the penitentiary.

The guard, tired, bored, smoked a thin cigarette which he held in a cupped hand down by his side, down by the shotgun. A sliver of grey smoke showed momentarily as it glided past his face and then disappeared into the gathering dark. The meal would be over by now, the guard was thinking, and the prisoners locked back into their cells or dormitories. His stomach grumbled a complaint, and he started to curse his luck at drawing this particular duty. There was a compensation, though. When he got to the kitchen, his plate would be piled higher than most anyone else's had been. He allowed himself a smile at the thought and moved the cigarette to his lips.

Joseph raised the hammer above his shoulder.

Gideon guided the shovel into the earth and lifted it clear.

The guard drew hard on the cigarette, then cupped it away, a small red glow between his fingers.

Gideon started to swing the shovel towards the pile of earth; this time he carried on swinging. The contents of the shovel were hurled hard into the guard's face and at the instant that the load had left the curved blade, Joseph smashed the hammer head down into the side of the kerosene lantern. The guard staggered sideways as the mixture of soil and stones showered across him, temporarily blinding him. His hand dropped the cigarette and grasped at the barrel of the shotgun, but his sudden movement had sent it falling away from him. He leaned over and blinked his eyes clear, only to discover that it was dark anyway. A shadow seemed to lunge towards him and he was torn between evading it and trying to retrieve the gun. He did neither. The underside of the shovel blade landed on the side of his head and smashed him against the brick wall. A muffled shout escaped from his mouth and a hand grabbed him, holding him off the ground. Joseph brought the hammer through a sharp arc.

They took up the shotgun, rolled the man over and pulled the pistol from his holster. Inside his pocket was a bunch of keys and, after the third attempt, Gideon found the one which unlocked the lengths of chain shackling their legs together. The chain gave them enough room to do their work; not enough for what lay before them. Both men left the shackles on the ground, but after a moment's thought, Joseph retrieved his and let it swing from his left hand. In his right he gripped the Colt .44. Gideon led the way with the shotgun.

Instead of heading directly to the kitchen, the two blacks ran around the rear of the governor's house and skirted the outbuildings until they reached the stables. The old timer who kept the guards' horses in trim, and who curry-combed the pair of bays that drew the carriage for the governor's wife, was enjoying a quiet game of cards with the stable boy. One sight of the shotgun in the light of the lamp that hung from the rafters, and cards were forgotten.

'Seven horses. The best. Get 'em saddled.'

'One sound an' you're both deader'n possum.'

It wasn't easy to fix harness with both hands shaking, but somehow it was done.

'Okay, now the rest. Soon as we're gone get 'em out in that corral. You hear shootin',' Gideon pointed the shotgun at the boy, 'you open the gate and drive 'em hard.'

Joseph started taking up reins. It was a forty-yard dash from the cells where Loughlin and Majors were imprisoned to the stables, but tethering the mounts anywhere closer was impossible.

'You all right, brother?' Joseph asked.

Gideon finished looping the last rein. 'Let's go.' He whirled round on the livery man and brandished the shotgun once more. 'These horses ain't here. Anythin' else goes wrong, I swear I'll ram this bastard down your straggly throat an' laugh while I pulls the trigger. You understand me?'

The old man was shaking so much he couldn't answer; it was clear enough that he understood. The stable boy's face was white as linen and he was awful close to throwing up.

'Okay.'

The two blacks set off towards the kitchens as fast as they could.

The side door was always kept locked and the trustee who was waiting for the extra work detail to return only unfastened it when the guard knocked and called his name. On this occasion, things were different. Joseph swung the hammer hard against the wood and the lock broke away; he leaned his shoulder against the door and it sprang back, splintering widely. The trustee was still turning in that direction, his warning shout still forming on his lips, when Joseph swung the chain that dangled from his left hand. It struck the man across the face, instantly drawing blood and knocking him back against one of the stoves. There was a clatter of pans and the chain swung a second time and wrapped around the trustee's neck, hauling him close. Joseph hit him in the stomach with the handle of the hammer, and when his head came sharply forward, he drove the top of the implement down into his skull.

Gideon had drawn the pistol from his belt and passed it to Levy, along with the bunch of keys. They knew that it would enable them to unlock the main doors to the dormitory in which Baptiste and Little Kinney were kept, but that it was useless to get into the condemned men's cells. Keys to those were restricted to the guards who worked that area alone.

Levy pointed at the cupboard to his right. 'In there. Sacks of supplies. I've been stashing 'em ready. There's a couple of bigger sacks loose at the back.' Again he pointed. 'Load 'em up an' get 'em ready.'

'Right,' called Joseph. 'Move out!'

Levy half-ran, half-hopped through the kitchen to the dining room, forcing himself to ignore the pain in his leg. Plenty of time to let that heal up later when they were in the clear. He unlocked the dining room door and hurried across fifteen yards of blackness until he was by the entrance to the first dormitory block.

Fumbling with the keys, he dropped the ring to the ground; anxious, he only retrieved it on the third attempt. The butt of the Colt pushed awkwardly into his stomach and he readjusted it. His tongue seemed to be made of fur; thick fur.

The key caught in the lock and refused to turn more than half an inch. More sweat pumped through Levy's pores; his breath caught low down in his throat. The keys were wrong. The whoring keys were wrong! The key turned another fraction then stuck. Levy was filled with thoughts, images of disaster. When he did finally get the door open the dormitory would be full, not of prisoners, but guards. Armed and grinning. Ready to blast him . . .

The heavy lock gave under continued pressure and Levy pushed the door back. No guards. Wire cages, all the way up to the roof, divided the long room into two sections. Bunk beds pushed close together; here and there a pair had been moved even closer by the inmates themselves. Levy's feet refused to move from where he stood. Couldn't.

A shout broke his thoughts, his inaction: Baptiste calling from the far end. What in God's name was he doing?

What?

Levy scurried around the first cage, a small figure, no more than five six, his shoulders rounded and the suggestion of a hump to his back; he seemed to have no neck worth speaking of. A round face with a squashed-up nose and blue-green eyes that looked permanently startled.

'Get this damn thing unlocked!'

Baptiste was standing close to the door, fingers pushing between the diamonds of wire mesh. Tall where Levy was short, broad and strong where Levy was merely misshapen. His eyes were dark and they glared at Levy with anger. Sweat showed clearly on his skin, on the stubble that fringed his beard and moustache.

'Come on!'

Levy made the connection at the third attempt, wondering where Kinney had got to, glancing round for him, not concentrating on what he was doing.

'Jesus Christ!'

But the door came back with a creak and suddenly Kinney was there, at Baptiste's shoulder. A dozen or more other prisoners were up and on their feet, moving to the cage door. Voices yelled, startled, jubilant. Baptiste turned fast, his left arm extended. Two men staggered back, one of them losing blood freely from his nose, the other with both hands to his face. Little Kinney pulled Baptiste through and slammed the door shut. The howl that went up was deafening.

The three men raced to the main dormitory door. The other cage was awake and aware now and men hurled themselves against the wire, rocking it, threatening to bring it down. Levy let the other two out into the darkness and this time his fingers were more certain on the keys.

'You reckon Tap's okay?' Kinney glanced over his shoulder in the direction of the condemned cells.

'We got about a minute to find out,' said Baptiste. 'If he ain't out and runnin' by then . . .'

He let his sentence trail off into the night. There was more to do than talk. The hounds were already beginning to bay inside their runs, bodies banging against the sides. Soon the guards would be out, roused from sleep and heading for the dormitory block to see what was happening. Baptiste wondered if they shouldn't take off straight away; maybe a minute was going to prove too long.

Joseph belly-crawled the last twenty yards to the foot of the tower. The lanterns spilled down a wide, slightly wavering pool of light, the edges of which shifted with the wind. Holding his breath, he pushed himself up to his feet and took the one step necessary towards the bottom of the ladder. The chain was wrapped around his left wrist, fingers holding it taut so as not to allow the links to clink against one another. The hammer was pushed down into his pants with the head jutting out above the waistband.

Joseph tested his weight against the first rung, holding the sides as steady as he could. There was very little movement, next to no noise. He allowed himself the beginnings of a smile and began, slowly, to climb. Ten rungs from the top, he stopped and leaned forward, flattening himself as much as he could. From the footsteps above he knew that the guard had got up from his stool and was pacing around. A moment later he heard the quick, sharp scratch of a match and a long intake of breath; the spent match was tossed over the side and fell past him, spinning and turning.

Still the man turned and turned again within the confines of his circle. Joseph was beginning to get the first twinges of cramp in his right thigh; he straightened the leg to an exaggerated degree and pressed the sole of his foot down on to the ladder as hard as he dare. The feeling stopped, held, began to disperse.

There was a scraping sound as the guard readjusted his stool and then sat back down.

Joseph allowed himself no smiles this time – nothing until it was done. All of it. The last section of the climb took him longer than all the rest; the seconds before he peered over the top were fraught with expectations of disaster. The guard was sitting, cross-legged, smoking; he was two-thirds turned away from Joseph, looking out over the compound and the roofs beyond. Joseph said a quick, brief prayer without a sound, without a single movement of his lips.

He held out his left arm and took careful hold of one end of the length of chain, letting it silently unwind. One leg crossed the parapet, one leg followed by another. He could smell the slightly acrid tobacco smoke, see clearly the reddened swelling of a boil at the side of the man's neck.

Joseph brought his arms up above his head as he darted close, swung them down as he stopped short of the stool. Pulling his arms outwards sharply he wrenched the chain hard around the guard's neck and jerked it back into his own stomach, choking off any attempt to cry out. The chain twisted and turned and tightened again. There were sounds of fought-for breath, wriggling, gasping sounds which were not loud enough to travel beyond the top of the tower.

Joseph looked down and saw the eyes beginning to bulge out from their sockets and the tongue, purplish, slide out from the mouth. The muscles in his own arms strained against the sheen of his skin. One more effort and he felt the guard go limp. The cigarette had fallen from his fingers and lay smouldering on the floor. Joseph trod it out and released the chain. He noticed with disgust that the man's boil had burst against it, several of the links smeared with a mixture of puss and blood.

He lowered the guard to the ground and took up his rifle, checking the load. Joseph sat down on the stool, silhouetted by the lamps on either side of him, but no detail of his appearance visible from below. He stared down at the condemned block and waited.

Gideon had found it more difficult than he had anticipated scaling the wall of the building and swinging his weight on to the roof. He was sure it had taken him longer than planned and, as he slid the shovel ahead of him, he hoped that Tap wouldn't understand his lateness as meaning something had gone seriously wrong.

But there hadn't been shooting, only the sound of the dogs that was now beginning to start up across the central compound. Perhaps it was still going to be all right. He moved along the roof bent low, making as little noise as possible until he reached the far end. Then he counted back and felt the tarpaulin with his fingers. The knife that Levy had given him in the kitchens had been small but now proved sharp. He needed little enough pressure to slide the blade through the tarpaulin and then tear it away, exposing the boards of the roof. Gideon grunted with satisfaction and stood back, inserting the blade of the shovel into the narrow gap between the boards. He leaned backwards, straining his weight against the handle, levering the wood away. Slowly, the long nails came up through the rafters and soon he was able to kneel down and use his hands to wrench the first plank free.

Immediately, he heard the soft hiss of a voice calling up from the darkness below.

Tap Loughlin and Lloyd Majors had been scraping and carving away at the stonework near the top of their cells at intervals throughout the whole day and the preceding night. Moments only before they heard the sound they assumed to be Gideon on the roof, the first breakthrough had come. Majors had chipped clear sufficient space for his end of the bar to be heaved up and finally free. Both men had breathed deeply; Majors had grinned and nodded – he had been the one to do it. Loughlin turned away and now his end of the heavy bar came out with comparative ease.

They shimmied along the bunks, rolling the wire and iron back far enough to allow them to climb through.

When Gideon prised away the first board there was a dim but definite shaft of light above them. Loughlin moved along to the right, positioning himself underneath the gap, which increased as another board was removed. Then something snaked down through and it was the Negro's arm.

Tap Loughlin grasped Gideon's hand and grasped his arm at the elbow. One second he was precariously balanced, the next he was swinging through space then being hoisted high enough to let go of Gideon and catch hold of the roof itself. In another moment he was straddling the gap, breathing the musky air, listening to the baying of the dogs.

'Hey!' Majors' shout reached them from below.

Loughlin and Gideon exchanged glances.

'What the hell's goin' on up there?'

Loughlin still hesitated. So easy to let Majors stink in his own juice. The voices of the other condemned men began to rage and storm around them. At any moment the entire prison would be roused.

Loughlin nodded towards Gideon. 'Get him up,' he said and started towards the end of the roof. Once he glanced up at the tower and his heart stopped momentarily, seeing a figure seated there, gazing down. A second later he realized it had to be the other Negro.

'Come on!'

Loughlin grasped the shotgun Gideon had leant against the wall. Figures moved through the semi-darkness off to the side and Tap recognized Baptiste's gruff voice. He glanced back and saw Majors and Gideon moving along in his wake. The sound of horses. A warning shout which was followed hard by a pistol being fired. Three men in the saddle leading four other mounts, sacks of supplies bouncing out from their flanks as they moved.

'Let's go!'

Another shout and three men were running from the direction of the guards' quarters, at least one of them firing aimlessly. Joseph moved to the edge of the tower and angled the rifle down. His shots came fast, the first couple flying wide, the next wounding one of the guards, startling the others. Tap swung up into the saddle; Majors grabbed hold of an animal's reins and it bucked away from him, alarmed, nostrils flaring.

'Joseph!' yelled Gideon, astride one horse and leading another. 'Get down here!'

He rode towards the tower, aware that more guards were racing towards them. Suddenly the darkness was pierced by flashes of gunfire, seeming – impossibly – to surround them. Joseph fired back from the tower, not knowing whether he was taking effect. He sprang back and descended the ladder as quickly as he could.

The night had gone berserk. Bells were ringing, and through them the shrill blasts of whistles. Off towards the dormitory block, there was a bright flickering as if part of the building had somehow been set ablaze. A guard sprinted close to the milling horses, intent upon getting to the dogs and releasing them. Scott Levy leaned well over in his saddle and followed his run, steadying the pistol as best he could. The first shot went wide, the second made the guard stumble, without apparently hitting him. The third left him clawing dirt, a bullet high in the back of his leg.

'Move out!'

Tap Loughlin's voice roared loud and he kicked into his horse's sides and whipped the reins down on to its neck. He urged the animal through a knot of men, uncertain if they were guards or other prisoners. A hand grabbed at his leg and tried to drag him from the saddle.

Joseph came fast alongside and the hammer swung in a wide arc. There was a crunch, hard and then soft, a shout and the man let go, falling away beneath the hooves of the others.

The escaping men turned hard past a group of outbuildings and the gate was less than eighty yards ahead. A solitary guard shuffled his way in front of it, lifting his rifle to his shoulder. Tap looped the reins round the saddle pommel and guided the horse with his knees. The shotgun was in both hands and the guard still hadn't fired. Wasn't going to. Faced with seven charging riders, he threw down his gun and ran. Too late to stop his finger against the triggers, Tap blasted both barrels of shot through the white-painted slats of the gate. Just in time he released the shotgun into his left hand, grabbed the reins with his right and leaned back in the saddle. He felt the animal start to jump beneath him and then they were down on the other side and galloping hard, hooves of the others thundering at his back.

Sounds of shooting, clamouring bells and strident whistles all faded until there was nothing left but the drumming of their own escape along the dirt-track road. Even Tap Loughlin's hatred for

Majors had evaporated in the excitement of their success. Free as the wind, and as far as he could tell not one of them had received so much as a scratch.

Loughlin swung in the saddle and raised a hand in triumph. Baptiste saw the gesture and responded in like manner. They would ride hard for the next couple of hours, until they came across some farm where they could steal fresh mounts. By daybreak they should be on their way out of the state: on their way to freedom. Above them the moon was as round and unreal as a silver circle stuck into a kid's picture book.

Three

Wes Hart had been to Fort Smith before and he didn't have a single good memory of it. On that occasion he'd ridden in with a US deputy marshal's badge pinned to his vest and a couple of prisoners in tow behind him. Kids had run along the street after him and men and women had turned from the boardwalk and stared. Not so many days later, Hart had stood in a crowded square in front of the courthouse and watched as Judge Parker's hangman had stretched the pair of them from lengths of best Kentucky hemp. One of the prisoners had been little more than a kid himself and it had taken him a long while to die. Dangling there, legs kicking while his stubborn breath slowly choked out of him. Hart had quit then, turned in his badge and ridden away, the remembrance bitter in his brain.

Now he'd ridden in with a freight wagon, supplies that had been in need of a driver who was handy with a gun in case anyone decided to take early delivery along the route. But the journey had been straightforward, untroubled. Hart had been well enough paid. He squashed his first instinct to turn right around and head back where he'd come from. With money in his pocket he had a hankering after a hot tub and a close shave, a steak so big that it flopped over the edges of the plate – and a bottle of whisky that didn't take the skin off your lips as it went past. Whatever else Hart thought of Fort Smith, he was the first to admit that it was the kind of town that afforded a man the chance to enjoy himself more than a little. As long as he could afford to pay for it.

The town was set out in regular patterns, the main streets wide and lined with trees; name plates had been stuck up which called them such-and-such avenue and even so-and-so boulevard. The stores had plate glass windows and were packed with goods; the streets were busy with folk wandering up and down, men in suits some of them, women who looked like the pictures Hart had seen often enough in company catalogues but seldom in real life. Children ran between the slow-moving wagons on the street, chasing one another with pretend guns fashioned from pieces of wood. A girl with long blonde ringlets and a gingham dress that flared out over a starched petticoat wheeled her hoop in a wide circle.

Hart rode between them, hardly an eye turning in his direction. There was no badge pinned to him now, nor were there any desperadoes roped or handcuffed to their horses behind him. He was a nobody, a cowboy, a drifter – just one more man with a horse and a gun and not a lot else.

He pulled on the rein and went down a narrow street running off the side. Midway down there was a sign that announced rooms for rent, clean linen and bath, fifty cents. It didn't take long for Hart to secure one for the night, take his horse along to the nearest livery, get back and ask the woman whose place it was to boil some hot water for him. The room was at the front, facing out on to a slender branched tree with leaves that were tinged with yellow. The mattress gave beneath his weight but not too much. The sheets were torn and then patched but clean right enough. There was an oval mirror above the chest of drawers and Hart stared into it, surprised by the amount of trail dirt that was smeared over his face and clogged into the corners of his eyes.

He tipped cold water from the enamel jug on the washstand into a broad china basin. He cupped the water into his hands and splashed it up into his face, shaking his head from side to side. In the mirror it was possible now to see the tanned skin of his lean face, taut across the high cheekbones; the faded blue of his eyes. It was the face of a man nobody would mistake for an inexperienced youngster; nor would anyone consider his prime years were behind him. He stood an inch over six feet and his frame was wiry and strong; it was doubtful if there was one pound of surplus flesh on his bones.

Recognizing himself at last, Hart turned away from the mirror and unbuckled his gun belt, hanging it over the brass rail at the foot of the bed. The belt was made from strong but supple leather, patterned with dust but evidently well cared for. The pistol in the holster was a Colt Peacemaker .45 and no ordinary one. The grip on the butt was made from mother-of-pearl carved with the Mexican emblem of an eagle gripping a snake tight between his claws and in his mouth.

Along with the dapple grey mare that Hart rode, that Colt was his most precious possession. He had killed a man out in Indian territory for stealing the mare; if there were anything more than that he could do to anyone who tried to take his gun away from him then he surely would.

Hart sat down on the edge of the bed and pulled off, with some difficulty, his scuffed and worn leather boots. Blood raced down his feet to his toes and tingled. There were large holes in the pair of outer socks that he wore, his toe was beginning to poke through those underneath. It passed through his mind that he might ask the woman if she'd darn them for him while he was soaking in the tub. He stood up and slipped off his brown leather vest, began to unbutton the thick wool shirt.

'Water's ready!'

Hart stepped out on to the landing, bare-footed, socks between the finger and thumb of his left hand.

'Bathroom's down below, through the kitchen. You'll have to lift the pans of water off the stove yourself, I can't manage heavy work like that any longer.'

She broke off abruptly, staring through wire-framed spectacles at the socks Hart was dangling in her direction.

'Is there some significance in that, young man?'

Hart grinned. It was a long time since anyone had called him young man, but he supposed this woman had the years to do it.

'I was wonderin' if . . .'

'If I'd kindly mend them for you, I guess.'

'Well, I figured . . .'

'That an old woman like me wouldn't have anything better to do with her time than push a darning needle through what seem to be a remarkably unpleasant pair of socks.'

Hart sighed and withdrew the socks. 'It don't matter,' he said shortly and went to walk past her.

'Now don't take on so!'

'I weren't taking on.'

'Huh! That's what I'd call it.'

Hart shrugged and continued along the landing. As he came level with her, she reached out a hand and took hold of the ends of the socks. For a few moments they stood, facing one another, each clinging to the holed, sweaty socks.

'Well?' she demanded. 'Are you going to let me have them or what?'

Hart let her have them.

'I suppose those things you're wearing wouldn't be any the worse for a wash.' She held her head back as she spoke, making the smell of stale sweat and riding dirt obvious.

Hart hesitated.

'You have got some other clothes you could wear while those are drying?'

''Cept pants,' admitted Hart.

'All right then. Though why I should put myself out I'm not really sure.'

She went towards the stairs, holding the socks as if they were infected. Hart ducked back into his room and pulled a creased but fairly clean shirt from his saddle bag, along with a pair of cut-off long johns. A few minutes later he was easing himself down into a hip bath of steaming water and his dirty clothes were headed for the back yard. Hart lay back for a while, just enjoying the warmth and the way it soaked the soreness out of his limbs. After that he reached on to the floor for a slap of soap and began to lather himself. He was attending to his arms when the door started to open.

'Hey!' Hart called out, thinking it must be the woman.

It was not.

The man was wearing a battered stetson that was angled down over his left eye near close enough to shut it out. A long moustache, grey at the ends where it met the jaw line and brown higher up, was the most remarkable feature of his face. Over a green shirt he was wearing an old buckskin coat that came past his hips. It was unbuttoned and hung loose, letting Hart see a good length of his gun belt, though not the pistol that was holstered at the right side. The only other thing to note about him was the six-pointed star pinned to the lapel of the coat, the words US MARSHAL engraved deep at its centre.

He stared down at the tub and snorted a half-laugh.

''Lo, Wes,' he said.

Hart nodded. 'Marshal.'

Already Hart was trying to figure out what the lawman wanted, how the hell he knew that he was there at all. There was only one way out of the room and that was the door and the marshal had placed himself between that and the tub. Hart's Colt was up in his room, hanging from the end of the bed. He didn't have to need it, only . . .

'You ain't forgot who I am, then?' said the lawman, with a faint smile to his face.

No: James F. Fagan, United States marshal and running-boy for Hanging Judge Parker. The man who'd run into Hart a year or so back in a one-eyed hole named Stillwater that later was to run deep in blood. Fagan was the one who'd persuaded him to ride as deputy, the man who'd sworn him in. It was at Fagan's feet – and Judge Parker's – that he'd hurled his badge in disgust.

'What is it, Fagan?'

'Just a few words.'

'Then they can wait till I finished here.'

Fagan shook his head slowly. 'You forget I'm a busy man.'

'My heart bleeds,' said Hart sarcastically.

Fagan laughed, an unpleasant sound. 'That ain't the kind of thing a man in your position ought to joke over.'

'My position bein' what exactly?'

Fagan brushed back the right side of his buckskin and let his hand fall close to the butt of his pistol. 'Your position bein' that you're bare-assed naked and your Colt's a long way from home.'

'That so?'

Fagan nodded.

'An' am I goin' to be needin' that Colt this visit?' asked Hart, his voice flat and hard.

The same smile spread across Fagan's face, his mouth curling at the edges, his eyes wrinkling. He moved his hand, left not right, and delved at the back of his coat. The gun he slid out from his belt was the pearl-handled Colt Peacemaker that was unmistakably Hart's.

'What . . . ?'

Fagan tossed the gun through the air in a slow, looping curve; Hart splashed his arm up through the water and caught the pistol at the first attempt. He turned it in his hand and sensed that something was not right. As he rested his thumb against the hammer, Fagan's smile became an outright laugh.

'You didn't reckon I'd leave it loaded, did you?'

Hart shook his head, glanced at the gun, set it down on the floor close to the base of the tub.

'Since when've you spent your time pussy-footin' round folks' rooms?'

'Since I needed to.'

'Meanin'?'

Fagan shrugged. 'Meanin' I had no way of knowin' you was soakin' your dirt off down here. I said before, all I wanted was a few words.'

'And my gun.'

'You got it back.'

'Empty.'

Fagan chuckled. 'You can be pretty bull-headed at times. And I didn't get to be forty-two by takin' chances.'

Hart let his mind run over what the peace officer had said. He tried to work out if there was anything in the past months that might have brought Fagan to take a professional interest in him, but he couldn't recall anything that might be considered specially unlawful. Not sufficient to interest Fagan, anyhow.

'What is it, Fagan? What are these words you want?'

'How long you fixin' to hang round town?'

'No longer'n I need to. Why? You tellin' me I ain't welcome?'

'I didn't say that.'

'For a man who was so damn anxious to see me, you didn't say a lot of anythin'.'

'Okay. Take it easy. I just got a message for you is all.'

'Message?'

'Man wants to see you.'

'He want to watch me scrub my back, too?'

'Very funny, Hart.'

'Not so damned bad. Now s'pose you spit it out and let me get on with my business here before this water cools off.'

Fagan nodded and moved a few feet further from the door. Hart didn't hear anyone else around, but he wouldn't have minded placing a ten-dollar bet that at least one of the marshal's deputies was hovering outside. Like the man said, he didn't get to be forty-two by taking chances.

'Man name of Grant. Banker. Got a big place up north of here. Outside of Cass. You know it?'

'Uh-uh.'

'You'll find it easy enough.'

'That's if I go lookin'.'

Fagan ignored him and carried right on. 'This Grant he wants someone who's good with a gun and ain't overfussy about usin' it. Someone he can pay to do a job and trust to see it through.'

Hart nodded. 'You told him 'bout me. What else d'you say?'

'I said you were for hire and you weren't cheap.'

'That all?'

'Said you were my deputy for a time. Handled yourself pretty good.'

'Thanks. Now you want to tell me what it's all about?'

Fagan shook his head, started to move back towards the door. 'He'll do that for himself. Malc Grant ain't the kind of a man who likes others to do his talking for him.'

Hart looked at Fagan keenly. 'This business,' he said, 'there wouldn't be nothin', let's say, illegal 'bout it, would there? That wouldn't be the reason why you're bein' as shy as a young girl 'bout to head off to her first dance?'

Fagan glowered, then grinned. 'Just remember, Hart, you're talkin' to a United States marshal.'

Hart nodded. 'I was.'

Fagan rested one hand against the door frame. 'When you get up there, tell him I sent you. That's a favour I might need to call back some time.'

'I'll tell him.' Hart splashed back in the tub and waves of water slopped over the edges on to the floor. 'If I go.'

Fagan had stepped out of sight: for a moment he stepped back. 'Next time you're takin' your yearly bath, be more careful where you leave that fancy Colt of yours.'

Hart stared at the lawman's sarcastic face, knowing that he was right. Not certain yet whether he'd take that ride north of Fort Smith up towards Cass and this Grant. He was choked to his craw with bankers and big ranchers and all kinds of investment men who were parcelling up the land and getting it to work for them, sitting back in soft leather armchairs with brandy and cigars the size of sixguns. Not even in the country some of them – France, Scotland, Germany. Hart had had his fill.

And yet . . .

Bringing in that freight wagon had paid him twenty dollars. Wearing a US deputy marshal's badge had brought seventy-five a month. To stay his own man he was going to have to sell his services to the highest bidder: and that more often than not meant working for folk he despised. Hart looked down at the surface of the tub, where the dirt was floating like thick grey scum across the water, sealing his body in. Angrily, he splashed it away and climbed out. By the time he'd towelled himself briskly down, his annoyance had tempered somewhat and he greeted the landlady with a hint of a smile and even a gruff thank-you as she handed him back his darned socks. Climbing the stairs he caught the smell of steak frying in the kitchen. Maybe the rest of the day wouldn't be as bad. He could forget about Grant – until the morning.

Four

Hart followed the meandering path of the Mulberry River north-east out of Fort Smith. Cass was the best part of a day's ride if he wasn't going to drive the grey and himself too hard, there didn't seem to be a great deal of point to that. Although the sun grazed through the clouds a few times, it remained overcast, a strong wind cutting down from the north and keeping Hart's eyes narrowed and the brim of his flat-crowned hat pulled well down. The Navajo chief's blanket that had been presented to him in gratitude by He Who Runs getting on twelve years back was draped diagonally across the top of his body and held in a knot below his left hip. Incongruously, he was also wearing his usual length of ragged woollen scarf which he pulled over the lower half of his face when the wind was strong enough to whip up dust. Scuffed leather gloves fitted tight on his fingers as he handled the reins.

He stopped several times, down by the Mulberry so that the grey and himself could drink and he could throw the cold water up into his face. Once, he loosened the animal's girth and took a piece of dried beef jerky from his bags, biting off a chunk and chewing it laboriously. He pulled out a bag of broken biscuits and shared them with the horse, the grey's breath hot against the palm of his hand.

Back in the saddle, Hart touched her lightly with his spurs and she stretched into a gallop, the ground thundering beneath them. Hart leaned low over the grey's neck, enjoying the sensation of speed.

'C'mon, Clay! C'mon!'

After a mile or so, horse and rider tired and reverted to a pace which alternated between a walk and a steady trot. The higher land, away from the river, was spotted with blackjack oak, narrow-trunked and between twenty and thirty feet high. The leathery leaves, green and brown, stood out strongly from the black bark. More than once Hart loosened the .44 Henry sheathed under the left-side flap of the saddle, only to realize that what was emerging from the uppermost branches was nothing more than a common crow.

The rifle stayed unused. On its opposite side, snug in a specially fashioned bucket holster, was Hart's sawn-off, a Remington ten-gauge with its twin barrels no more than fourteen inches in length. It didn't aim worth a dud two-bits, but in a crowded space and up against more than one man it was invaluable. Hart's armoury was completed by an Indian knife, double-bladed and so well honed that it would slice through skin at the merest touch. This hung from the saddle pommel in a fringed buckskin sheath. At present. When he figured it might come in useful, he hung it round his neck beneath his shirt. It was often the last card and a good one.

The sky was beginning to darken further when he came up to a wagon travelling the same road. With two flea-bitten mules drawing it and too much weight on board, it was going near slow enough to be heading backwards.

Hart rode up alongside carefully and with a warning shout of greeting, anxious not to startle whoever was up front into any hasty action.

He needn't have worried.

The driver was slumped foward on the bench seat, the reins loosely looped over the tall brake pole letting the mules find their own pace. He was a burly-looking man, the black coat he was wearing fashionable and smart perhaps twenty years earlier. The top hat that he wore at a rakish angle on his head was losing part of its crown and there was one cigarette burn through the near side. A pair of ageing brown boots sat on the seat beside him and his feet were calloused and bare.

Hart looked back along the canvas side of the wagon:

Seymore Hardcastle's Cure-All.

The letters were shakily formed and already fading, elongated red lines down the yellowing canvas. Hart glanced back at the driver. It looked as if the one thing his cure-all didn't tend to was sleeping sickness. He used his knees to bring Clay close alongside and reached out his left hand towards the unmoving man.

Even through the rattle of the wheels he heard the unmistakable sound of the hammer being drawn back, a triple click that left him no alternative other than to freeze where he was.

After a couple of seconds in which nothing else happened, Hart slowly turned his head. The barrel of a gun poked through the folds at the front of the wagon to meet him. Hart looked at it evenly, a small pistol, likely a .38. He held his breath. Still nothing happened. The mules and his own horse kept on at the same pace.

'No call to be alarmed,' said Hart finally. 'I was just . . .'

'Fixin' to steal Seymore's wallet,' the voice finished for him.

With a start Hart realized that the person holding a gun on him was a woman; it surprised him but it didn't make him feel any easier.

'Ma'am, that ain't so. I . . .'

'Don't ma'am me!'

'I was just tryin' to explain what I was doin'. And if I don't know your name, how can I . . .'

'Never mind that. Just the rest and make it convincing.' She sounded about as pleasant as a wasp caught inside a poke bonnet.

'I was fixin' to wake him is all.'

'What for?'

'Ask directions?'

'Huh!' The snort was loud and effusive. The pistol trembled a little but not much. Hart was trying to picture the woman in his mind but it wasn't easy.

'Maybe,' said Hart placatingly, 'if you was to come out from there, I could ask you instead.'

This brought a slight shuffling, but no direct response. Hart looked aside at the driver, surprised that he should sleep so soundly through it all, and realized he was no longer asleep at all. True, his eyes were still closed beneath the brim of the top hat and he hadn't altered his slumped position, but a small working of the mouth told Hart that he was indeed awake. Likely had been for some time, waiting to see which way things sprung.

Hart leaned back in the saddle, straightening up. The .38 followed his movements, but nothing more. At last, the folds of the canvas were pushed back to reveal a woman of considerable size, a tattered fur coat draped over her ample shoulders. Her face was round but pretty, despite the fact that she was some way past what most folk would agree to as young. Her hair was an indeterminate brown and piled indecorously on top of her head, wisps falling down past her ears and across her forehead. None of this was particularly surprising.

There was more. In her left arm she cradled a small baby, well under a year, Hart guessed. The child had evidently fallen asleep suckling the woman's left breast and now lay against it, mouth slightly open and a thin trail of spittle running down from the large brown nipple. Her right arm was folded at the elbow against her hip and it was this hand that held the gun. Steady.

'Myra!' gasped the driver, shaking himself properly awake and turning round. 'What in the good Lord's name are you doin' showin' yourself off to all an' sundry like that?'

In case she missed the drift of what he said, the man nodded his top hat in the direction of her exposed chest.

'Seymore,' she answered quickly, never taking her eyes off Hart, 'in the first place I have serious doubts if the good Lord would be shocked by my body and in the second there ain't no all and sundry, just this no-account who was on the point of liftin' that wallet of yours out of your pocket.'

Hardcastle patted his side pocket to make sure the wallet was still in place.

''Course,' she went on, 'that ain't what he says he was doin'. He says he wanted to ask some questions.' The look on her face and tone of her voice made it very clear just how much she believed him: not at all.

'One question,' said Hart. 'That's all. Let me get it asked and then I'll be ridin' on.' He looked at the woman, waiting for a response. 'How's that?'

She shrugged her shoulders and the baby whimpered a little and his mouth closed over her breast. 'You got a tongue in your head.'

Hart nodded and turned towards the driver. 'Feller name of Grant. Got a place close by here. Up near Cass. Pretty big by all accounts. Wondered if you knew exactly where.'

Hardcastle chewed the inside of his mouth a little, spat out over the rear of the mules and wriggled in his seat. 'Mile ahead,' he said eventually, 'river forks an' main stream heads on towards Cass. Follow the other up into the hills. Grant's place is up through the woods there. Only rode up there the once, but you can't miss it. Nothin' else around, not like that anyways. Big an' . . .'

'Seymore,' the woman interrupted, 'he don't want a description, just where to find it.'

The man looked at her grudgingly and set his head so sharply to one side that it seemed as if his hat might tumble off. As it was it contented itself with leaning more precariously than ever.

'Much obliged,' said Hart, pulling the grey clear of the wagon and touching his fingers to the underside of his own hat. 'I'll leave you to your journey.'

The woman didn't lower the pistol until Hart was a good hundred yards along the trail. As she did so, the child awoke and began to cry; she set down the gun and started to stroke its curly head. Hardcastle made a face as the noise set up, readjusted his top hat and unlooped the reins from the brake, shaking the mules into something more consistent with movement. Soon Hart and the grey were little more than a facing cloud of dust towards the horizon.

The house was in a wide clearing, oaks and a few aspens in a high curve at its back and sides. It was a wide single-storey building and carting all the necessary materials up through the woods must have cost enough to have built a dozen places elsewhere. Above a brick foundation that came a foot or so off the ground, the main structure was of wood, white-painted boards that were beginning to look a little weather-beaten towards the corners. The roof sloped up gradually and was tiled, with a pair of chimneys towards either end. What struck Hart most was the front, which consisted of a high arch of white brick at the top of a broad flight of five steps. On each side of the arch, wooden railings formed the front of a long porch. There were tall windows beyond the porch, smaller ones behind, each divided into small squares of glass. Smoke spiralled lazily up from both chimneys, turning away in the wind towards the trees behind. There was some thirty yards of grass out front, cut so close that it looked like somebody's daily task. Hart bet it wasn't Grant's.

This side of the grass there was an iron fence, no more than a couple of feet high. The tops of the railings were bent into symmetrical curves and the narrow gate at the centre was part open. If you came up on anything more than a single horse, Hart figured you had to find another way in. He lightly touched the grey's flanks and moved her through the gap, tipping back the brim of his stetson as he did so. For a big place there didn't seem to be much sign of life.

A little way out from the porch, he reined in. There was a figure standing up close to the window at the far left, girl or woman, Hart couldn't be certain. She seemed to hang against it, her print dress stuck to the glass. Her head was lowered, fair hair falling down to cover her face. She didn't move and, for a few moments, neither did Hart. Then he shifted Clay on towards the house.

Dismounting, he took the reins and looped them over the wooden railings at the porch front. He was two steps up when the heavy oak door swung slowly back and he was staring down the barrels of an American Arms shotgun. The man behind it bulked out the doorway, the vest of his dark grey suit straining and spotted with cigar ash. His face was round and with a tendency to hang jowls like an overweight and overfed pedigree dog. The eyes were almost shuttered in by creases and folds of fat but through all that they were bright enough. His hair was iron grey, harder and darker than the suit, almost the darkness of the railings by the gate.

Hart looked at the man, taking it all in, glancing at his hands, the way they gripped the gun. The fingers were fleshy and the backs sprouted hair generously. The nails were a little too long, a little too well polished. But the hands grasped the shotgun firmly enough and from that range he wasn't about to miss.

'State your business fast,' he said with a growl somewhere at the back of his throat. 'We don't take on no hired hands, don't give handouts and we ain't buyin' a damn thing.'

Hart felt a tendency to smile, which he overcame. 'Name's Wes Hart,' he said.

'Never heard of you.'

'Well, okay,' shrugged Hart. 'That don't matter none.'

'Then what in God's name . . . ?'

'The marshal said you might want to see me.'

'Why should I . . . ?'

'I don't know and he didn't say. If it's all a mistake, all I've lost is a day's ride.' Hart was turning away when the man's voice stopped him.

'You always interrupt a man that way?'

'If it means gettin' things closed quicker.' Hart was looking up the steps, his body still facing back down.

'It don't show a lot of respect,' snarled the man.

Hart shrugged his shoulders again, lightly this time; he came round to face the shotgun and took another step towards it. 'No,' he said, his voice tightening, 'it don't, does it?'

'Specially in the face of a gun.'

Hart nodded. 'That's right.'

'You're not frightened?'

'If you were going to use it, you'd have done so by now. Less'n I try to get past you and into the house without bein' asked, I don't reckon you'll use it now.'

Hart watched as the overweight face went through a few fleshy contortions which suggested that the man was thinking something over. His fingers had slackened their grip on the shotgun and Hart could have taken it from him right then, except that there no longer seemed to be any point. He tried to see inside the house, but there was little eye space between the man's body and the door frame.

'You're used to facing down a man with a gun?'

Hart looked back squarely. 'If I have to.'

'And you say the marshal sent you?'

'Fagan. United States Marshal James Fagan. I got the impression from him that you were looking for a man to do a job of work.'

The eyes, deep in the florid face, flickered. 'A gunman?'

'A regulator.'

The round face nodded, loose folds of fat under the chin wobbling on to the neck. 'Fagan recommended you, that it?'

Hart shrugged. 'Looks like it. I rode as his deputy a while back.'

'He fired you?'

'I turned in my badge.'

'Why?'

Hart hesitated slightly. 'Seemed a good idea at the time.'

'And now?'

'Still seems a good idea.'

The eyes were staring at the Colt in its holster, off to the side of the Indian blanket. A lot of assessing was going on, decisions being made which left less room for turning back. Eventually, the man lowered the shotgun until it was clasped against his left side. He stood to one side and prodded his empty hand towards the door.

'We'll talk inside.'

Hart let his eyes turn towards the end window but the angle was too acute to see whether or not the figure was still close by the squared panes.

Inside was wooden boards, wide and polished to a dull shine. Hand-woven rugs, some with Indian designs, were set here and there without apparent pattern. Doors led off in three directions from the hallway, two closed and the third open. It was through this that the man walked and Hart followed. The room they entered was long and high-ceilinged, three unlit kerosene lamps hanging at intervals. There were more rugs, furniture which had the appearance of being shipped upriver from St Louis or even New Orleans and then freighted overland. The chairs were fat and comfortable and upholstered in leather. A round table shone with a reddish sheen and the yellow and blue bowl at its centre was piled high with fruit. Above the fireplace there was a framed portrait of two children, a boy and a girl. The girl was sitting down, a bunch of gold flowers held in her lap; the boy, a lick of fair hair falling across his forehead, stood beside her, one hand resting lightly on her shoulder in a manner which suggested both love and protection.

Logs were burning in the grate and the smell was sweet in the room.

'Malcolm Grant.'

Hart took a firm grasp of the fleshy hand. 'Like I said, Wes Hart.'

'You'll take a drink?'

Hart nodded. 'Sure.'

'Whisky okay?'

'I guess your whisky's fine.'

They sat in armchairs at either side of the fire, tasting the good malt liquor Grant had had imported from Europe and talking of nothing very much. Grant was sounding him out, learning as much as he could and giving away very little about himself. Hart more or less relaxed, told the banker pretty much what he guessed he wanted to know. Out through the wide rear window, Hart could see a couple of long, low outhouses, one of which had smoke coming from a tin stack jutting out of the roof. He figured that was where the hired help lived. There was a small corral off to the right with some fine-looking stock, and back of that were some freshly planted fruit trees.

Hart kept in the back of his mind the thought that the woman from the window might come in at any moment and interrupt, but she didn't. His eyes caught the portrait and he got to thinking whether the person he had seen was the girl holding the flowers or her mother.

Grant caught the direction of his glance, maybe even interpreted his thoughts.

'My children,' he said, lowering his voice to something approaching veneration. 'Katherine and Lewis.'

Hart said something complimentary about the picture and waited for Grant to continue.

This he did only after draining his glass and refilling it, offering the bottle to Hart, who shook his head and declined.

'This has to do with them, with Katherine and . . . Lewis. The matter at hand.'

He was finding it difficult to talk about and Hart watched him struggling with it, an oversize fish snagged on the end of a line and unable to shake the hook.

A little more whisky helped; it was good whisky.

'Only months back when we were living in Fort Smith.' He glanced up at Hart. 'I had certain banking interests there.' And away again. 'Lewis was escorting Katherine home. They took a short cut off the main street. It may not have been sensible, but shouldn't a man expect his children to be able to walk around their home town without fear of . . . ?'

Grant's body shuddered. He set the glass to his lips and it rattled against his teeth as he drank. The eyes seemed to have withdrawn even deeper into his head and they were no longer bright. A log toppled down in the fireplace and a flurry of sparks flew up.

'My daughter, Katherine, she was attacked by a man. I don't need to tell you the nature of the . . . Lewis, he went to her defence. For his courage the cowardly bastard rewarded him with a knife between the ribs. Having killed my son, he returned to my daughter.' He stared across the room. 'Mr Hart, they were little more than children. Brave, strong children. Strong and . . .' His voice trembled a fraction and he glanced above the fireplace. '. . . beautiful.'

Hart leaned his weight back in the chair; the leather creaked a little under him. He set his almost empty glass down on the polished floor.

'Your daughter, was she . . . ?'

'She lived, Mr Hart. If that's what you can call it. She lived, she lives now. Lives here.'

Grant stood up and walked briskly towards the window, turning back into the room, his hands clenched by his sides. Behind his bulk the sky was beginning to darken, the sun was a glowing, stretching red across his shoulders.

'I sold the house in town and moved up here. I thought, away from where it had happened, Katherine would recover. Gradually, she would forget what had taken place.'

Hart's mind went to the figure against the window, the unmoving, bowed body, the lowered head.

'Her mother died when she was a young girl, no more than seven. Perhaps if she had still been alive and Katherine had someone to talk to . . .'

Grant broke off and started to pace restlessly about the room; he picked up the bottle and set it down again, unused; toyed with a cigar box and left that also.

'She hasn't spoken to me since it happened. Never more than a few words. And every time she looks at me . . .' Grant turned heavily towards the window and Hart watched as he fought to control his emotions, hands opening and closing, his breathing clearly audible across the room. 'Every time she looks at me . . .' The words were only just loud enough to make out, fragmented and halting. '. . . I can see in her face that she's blaming . . . blaming me . . . for what happened.'

His body hunched forwards and Hart thought for one moment that he was going to break down, but instead he whirled round and slammed one hand, bunched into a huge fist, hard down into the palm of the other. Veins on his neck were standing out through the fat. His eyes strained through the hoods of loose flesh.

'The evil bastard who did this to her!' Grant strode towards the fire, towards Hart but not looking at him, looking only at the picture hanging from the wall. 'The evil bastard!'

Hart waited until his breathing grew more controlled and his body was beginning to relax. Then he said: 'You want me to find him. Then what?'

Grant didn't move, made no sign that he had heard.

'I said what do you want me to do with him then?'

Grant looked round hard. 'After what I've told you, you still have to ask that?'

'You want a killer, go find someone else.' Hart's voice was flat, unyielding.

'Even the least of men will shoot down a wild dog,' snarled Grant.

'That ain't in question.'

'Then what the hell is?'

Hart stood up, facing the banker down until the puffy eyelids blinked and the eyes looked away. 'You want me to catch up with him, I'll do my best. But unless he don't leave me no alternative, I'm takin' him in for trial.'

Grant rocked back on his heels a little and when Hart thought he was about to lose his temper he surprised him by throwing back his head and roaring out a monstrous laugh.

'Trial! That's a poor joke, Mr Hart. A poor damned joke!'

'I don't understand.'

'No, you don't. He already stood trial. Up there in front of Judge Parker and sentenced to be hung. He was waiting for his time in the State Penitentiary only he didn't wait that long.'

'Broke out?'

'Along with half a dozen others.'

'How long back?'

'Near on a week.'

It was Hart's turn to walk around, stretch his legs. Grant offered him a drink and this time he refused; waited while the banker lit himself a cigar, snipping off one end and throwing it into the fire.

It was almost completely dark outside now, the remnants of the sun were smeared across the horizon like blue berries left to rot and decay. Hart thought he heard footsteps, quiet, outside the door, but he couldn't be certain. Grant, at least, gave no sign.

'The marshal . . .' Hart began.

'Fagan'll do what he can. But he's one man and there aren't deputies enough to help out. Besides, he's got other things to tend to. I want a man who can find Lloyd Majors and keep lookin' till he does.'

Hart nodded. 'You rememberin' my conditions?'

'If you can't find excuse enough to gun him down like he deserves, bring him back to me. I'll string him up over the front door with my own hands.'

Hart believed he would.

'You'll do it?' Grant asked.

'Seventy-five dollars a week and five hundred when I bring him in.'

Grant tapped his finger ends against the mantel, glanced up at the portrait.

'Dead or alive.'

'I told you how it'd be.'

'All right. We've got a deal.'

Grant put out his hand and this time Hart noticed that it was clammy with cooling sweat.

'You'd best stay here tonight. There's a spare bunk out back. I've got three men working for me and one of them's bringing a load of wire back from Fort Smith. I'll take you out.'

Hart shook his head. 'Don't bother. I'll make my own introductions.'

Grant nodded. 'Suit yourself.'

Almost at the door, Grant called Hart back. 'I don't have to tell you how important this is to me, Mr Hart?'

'No. You don't.'

'Good.' He moved a few paces away from the fire. 'I have breakfast a little after sun-up. If you'd care to join me.'

Hart nodded. 'Sure.'

He didn't suppose the banker's breakfasts were half bad – and a good meal inside him at the start of the day would stand him in good stead. He was going to have plenty enough to do before even he could begin to track Majors down. There were questions enough that wanted asking, possibilities to be considered, assessed.

Stepping out through the door, Hart stiffened at a sharp scraping sound and swung his head high. Something scuttled along in the guttering of the tiled roof. Below and off to the left, the light from a lantern cast a young woman's silhouette on to the window. Hart pulled the Indian blanket tighter about him and strode off towards the bunkhouse. There was a light burning there too, fainter, smudged by the tainted glass. Inside, two men were playing cards with a dog-eared pack. Their hands moved towards their weapons as Hart knocked and entered. Quickly he explained who he was and they relaxed and pointed out his bunk, offered him coffee from the warmed-over grounds on the small stove set at the centre of the long room. Half an hour later, Hart was laying on the bunk, thinking about the coming day; fifteen minutes more and he was asleep, mouth slightly open, the sound of relaxed breathing quiet as the shuffle of cards.

Five

Any animosity between Tap Loughlin and Lloyd Majors had become submerged in their mutual need to escape; once outside the penitentiary the important thing was to stay free and clear. Before the gang of men had been on the road two hours they had raided a farm close to the northern trail. There had been five folk inside, a man and woman, two young kids and a hired hand. The farmer had got a few knuckles on his right hand busted reaching for a rifle and there was the beginnings of a large bruise alongside his jaw. No one else had resisted over much. The woman had screamed and Majors had started in towards her, but Tap had read the trouble and intercepted him, slapping the woman across the face hard. She hadn't thanked him for it, but from the look that had been coming into Major's eyes, she should have done.

They'd added to their supplies to the tune of some coffee beans and fresh baked bread, dill and onion and smelling fine enough for the gang to eat a loaf there and then. There had been enough clothing of the farmer's and the hired hand's to go round everyone except Joseph and Gideon, who were too big to fit their limbs into anything there.

Sun-up had found them well north of the Petit Jean, with no evidence of a posse and no sound of baying hounds on their track. A fire had cooked breakfast and coffee and the men had talked about what they were going to do.

''Fore we do anythin' else,' said Baptiste, 'we go to get us some money.'

Majors laughed and leaned back on his haunches. 'That's easy enough, ain't it?'

'How come?'

'Aren't you fellers hold-up artists? Ain't that what you're so damned good at? All we got to do is sit here and wait for you to come back with the goods.'

Tap Loughlin pushed his boot against the edge of the fire and flames stirred up, licking around the top of the pan in which the coffee was simmering. 'You seem to be forgettin' somethin', Majors.'

'Yeah?' Majors leered forward. 'An' what might that be?'

'We had an agreement.'

'We did?'

'Yes, we did.'

Loughlin was standing straight and the pistol he'd taken from the farm was jutting up from his belt, the butt hard against the flat of his belly. Baptiste had a shotgun close by his hand and Joseph was toying with another. It wasn't clear that the two blacks would side with Loughlin if it came to a showdown, only pretty likely; there wasn't any doubting which way Tap's own men would jump, though. For all that, Majors didn't appear in the least afraid.

'Maybe you'd better remind me,' he said, tauntingly. 'My memory, it ain't so good.'

'Okay,' said Loughlin, his fingers so close to touching the gun. 'We get out, we split up. That's it.'

'Maybe I like it hanging around?' grinned Majors.

'And maybe I don't!'

Loughlin glanced at Baptiste and noticed that the shotgun was now resting across his knees, finger inside the trigger guard. Joseph still didn't seem to have made up his mind for certain, but Scott Levy had his hand less than a couple of inches away from the pistol in his pocket.

'Look, Loughlin,' said Majors, leaning forward, the smile disappearing from his face and his voice becoming serious, 'we just agreed that we're not going to get much further without a few dollars in our pockets, ain't that right?'

'Go on.'

'Let's say we hang together until that's over.'

'Until we've ridden in some place and done it for you.'

'That's not what I mean.'

'What then?'

Majors pushed his hands down into the ground, leaving clear, heavy impressions when he lifted them away moments later and brushed them against his pants. 'We pick the spot. You do that. It's your game. Ride in together. Share the risks. Share the money. Then I'll ride out.'

'What's wrong with you gettin' rich on your own account?' put in Baptiste.

'I said, it ain't my game. If I come in with you and get set up, that'll be it. Better if none of us gets caught an' if I've got money I can head off into Indian territory with no problems.'

Loughlin gave it a few seconds thought.

'Let him ride with us,' said Gideon. 'One more gun ain't goin' to harm none.'

'That's right,' agreed Joseph.

Loughlin reluctantly agreed. The next town they arrived at, a couple of them would ride in and check it out. If everything seemed quiet enough, they would hit the place hard, get what they could and then that would be the last they'd ever see of Lloyd Majors.

'And one thing's clear,' added Loughlin.

'Yeah?'

'This is my show. I do the callin'.' He pointed a finger directly at Majors, who was grinning again almost fit to bust. 'You got that?'

'Sure, sure. I understand. You call the shots.' Laughing, Majors turned his back on Loughlin and reached down for the coffee.

Peebles' Halt was a scattering of buildings on the southern banks of one of the narrow rivers that ran down from the higher ground of Magazine Mountain into the Petit Jean. The river was called the White Fork by some folk and the Snake by others. Peebles' Halt itself was named after the trading post and drinking place that had been started up there by a Scotsman from Aberdeen who sported a totally bald head and a taste for whisky, leather-bound volumes of travel writing and sheep. Gradually, other folk had settled round the original building, some on purpose, others more or less by chance. Peebles himself had sold his first place just a year to the day before a twister tore it down. He built a two-storey saloon and store with its own windmill out back and a brick store house equipped with a padlock.

Pulled in around there was a blacksmith who ran the livery stable; a barber who doubled as doctor and dentist both; an undertaker who baked bread and pies and charged travellers ten cents to wash off in his tin bath which he kept between the unused coffins. There was another store, which specialized in saddles and belts and ammunition. A laundry which functioned as the nearest thing to a whorehouse – when there weren't enough dirty shirts and sheets to pay the bills, the one-eyed Chinaman who ran the place sent his half-caste daughter down to Peebles' place to drum up a little extra trade. Once she'd lured a customer back to the laundry room and he'd got rid of his clothes, it wasn't unknown for the Chinaman to take them away and give them a quick wash, adding that charge to the bill.

What Peebles' Halt didn't boast was a bank. None of the folk that lived there ever seemed to have money enough long enough for any bank to do worthwhile business. There was a lot of trading going down, a month's washing set against feed and keep for a team of horses, two sacks of flour in exchange for a couple of dozen apple pies. Actual bills and silver pieces didn't change hands any too often.

The only person thought to have real money, of course, was Peebles. Why else would a man have a wagon load of bricks shipped in and build himself a store house and then fit a padlock to it, if he didn't have money locked away inside?

There couldn't be any other explanation.

Baptiste clicked his tongue sharply and pulled his horse alongside Loughlin's, the pair of them heading in from the river and passing the first buildings of the settlement. Fashioned from a mixture of sods and odd planks of wood and a couple of sheets of tin, they sure didn't amount to very much. Didn't give the impression of a community owning a lot of wealth.

'We're wastin' our time here,' said Baptiste. 'We ought to ride on right now.'

Loughlin nodded. 'Maybe. Maybe.'

He glanced sideways at the small figure of an Oriental-looking girl scurrying along the side of the street with a bundle of washing, almost as high as herself, balancing on her head.

'Long time in that cell, weren't it?' said Baptiste, also looking at the woman.

'Uh-huh.'

'You reckon it's true?' Baptiste asked, touching Loughlin on the arm to get his attention.

'How's that?'

'You know, what they say 'bout how them China girls is built.'

'Built?' blinked Loughlin.

'Yeah,' said Baptiste enthusiastically. 'The way their . . .'

The sound of a single pistol shot interrupted him and both Loughlin and himself swung towards the noise, hands reaching for their own guns. The laundry girl staggered on a few paces, the bundle of washing wobbling and shaking until it slowly toppled off her head and down into the dirt of the street.

Thirty yards away, a ragged man stepped out from beside a shack and hurled the lifeless form of a black and white dog into the middle of the street. There was an old Colt Navy in his left hand and a little smoke was still drifting from the end of the long barrel.

Baptiste and Loughlin exchanged glances and relaxed. The Chinese girl was scrambling around on the ground, retrieving the pieces of soiled laundry that would now have to be washed again.

'You know,' said the man who had just shot the dog, stepping out in front of the two riders, 'that blasted animal never gave a thank-you for a thing in all his life.'

Loughlin mumbled something and pulled on the reins, eager to move round both man and dog and be away.

'Brung him up since he was a pup an' fed him good, times even when there weren't enough food for myself, and still he never acted like he was grateful.'

He waved his pistol at Baptiste, who ducked his head away and swung his horse wide, pushing it to catch up with Loughlin. There were a few more people on the street now, drawn out by the man's clamorous whining.

'. . . put a bone down an' he bit me in the leg. Blast him! In the leg. All the thanks I ever got . . .'

When both men looked back, the man was on his knees beside the dead animal, the tatters of his coat trailing in the dirt of the street. His head was shaking from side to side and there were tears running down his face.

'Makes me thirsty,' said Baptiste. 'How 'bout we stop over there?'

Over there was Peebles' two-storey saloon and store, the sails of the windmill turning in the wind out back of it. Between the windows, unsteady letters proclaimed PEEBLES HALT in red paint that was flaking away here and there. There was only one window at the bottom, but that was wider and stuffed full with boxes and tins and barrels, most of them opened up and used to display the goods they contained: shoes and shirts and socks and cans of beans and packets of biscuits and rice and buttons and bandages. Inside, two walls were covered from floor to ceiling with goods stacked on warped shelves, on upturned crates, upon one another. Huddled together were tubs of galvanized staples, sheets of corrugated iron roofing; silver grey cotton and wool camp blankets; twenty-four dozen extra-chiselled flat-bristle flowing varnish brushes, two inches in width; a gross of nickel-plated raw horn dressing combs, five and a half inches long and one inch deep; seven-jewel, No. 1 movement, nickel watches in dustproof screw bezel filled cases, guaranteed for one year to keep perfect time; featherweight green transparent eyeshades with self-adjusting elastic ribbon; pairs of extra seamless three-ply cotton socks with four-ply heels and toes and ribbed tops; an assortment of bits and augers and chucks and reamers, nails and screws, hammers and chisels, taper files and wood rasps.

Loughlin and Baptiste were stopped in their tracks inside the door, the abundance of goods overwhelming them. That much of it was coated with a thick layer of dust, and that some items were beginning to take to themselves a hint of mildew and damp rot, didn't make it any less impressive.

Baptiste pushed his hat forward on his head and let out a low whistle. He was used to coming across such places in New Orleans, but out here in the middle of Arkansas, in a little two-bit place that couldn't even call itself a town without boasting overmuch . . .

'Drink, gents?'

Peebles himself was behind the bar, a fancy waistcoat with an embroidered front worn over a cream-coloured shirt that puffed out some at the sleeves. It looked as if he'd been helping himself to the best of his unsold goods and hadn't bothered overmuch about which sex they'd been designed for.

'Passin' through?'

The two men nodded and took and paid for their glasses of beer, fingering a good head of froth away on to the bar top.

'Headin' for Fort Smith, I guess?'

Tap Loughlin nodded again and half-turned his back. The only other occupants of the room were a hump-backed old timer who was sitting as close to the stove as he could without burning himself and a ginger and white cat with one ear missing.

'Ain't nowhere for most folk to go. Only Fort Smith. Round these parts, that is.'

An uneasy silence fell over the room. Loughlin and Baptiste downed their glasses and asked for refills, taking them off to a table pitched between stove and bar. Peebles watched them for a while, cursing them inside his head for being too damned stand-offish to pass the time of day. After a short while, he began sorting out the bottles racked beneath the counter and Baptiste and Loughlin got their heads together.

'If we was after pickin's,' said Tap Loughlin, 'we got us the wrong place. I don't see how there's more than fifty dollars in this whole damn settlement.'

Baptiste nodded. 'Reckon you're right. Less'n we was interested in settin' up store for ourselves.'

Tap half-smiled and glanced over his shoulder at the stock. 'That's true enough. He sure don't believe in wastin' any space, does he?'

Baptiste swallowed some more beer and wiped his sleeve across his mouth. 'What then? Tell the boys to give this place a miss an' ride on?'

Tap considered it for a few moments. 'Sure ain't worth no seven men ridin' in here, that's a fact.'

Baptiste nodded, drained his glass and set it down on the table with a crisp clip that was loud enough to make the old timer shift his arm and grunt and for the cat to raise its one ear. Peebles glanced over the top of the bar and then ducked back down when he saw it wasn't an order for more beer.

'Not so fast,' said Tap, leaning over and detaining the other man with a hand to his arm.

'What d'you mean?'

Loughlin nodded backwards. 'How much longer we intendin' to ride round this country with a couple of niggers wearin' prison clothes?'

Baptiste flicked a fleck of froth from his lips and his eyes brightened. Both men stood at the same time. They explained to Peebles what their requirements were in the way of dungarees and work shirts, socks and a couple of pairs of heavy-duty boots.

'Real big fellers, these friends of yours,' said the store owner.

Tap grinned at the thought. 'Real big,' he agreed.

Peebles finished pulling out what they wanted and wrapped the clothes in two large sheets of brown paper and tied them round with string.

'You'll take the boots separate?' he asked, arming a little sweat from the top of his bald head.

'Sure,' smiled Tap.

Peebles smiled back, pleased to be getting so much custom from a couple of drifters who hadn't seemed about to buy anything more than a few beers. He made a quick addition sum in his head and was even more pleased with himself that he got it worked out so fast.

'That'll be . . .'

And that was when he saw the pistol in Tap Loughlin's hand.

'. . . thirty dollars an' . . .'

But Tap was shaking his head and Baptiste already had the boots in one hand, holding them by the linked laces, and was pulling the parcel towards his chest with the other.

'We're a little out of ready cash right now,' explained Tap, enjoying the man's discomfort and surprise, 'so we'll just take these on credit.'

Peebles stammered a few words which didn't amount to very much. Neither the old man nor the cat had as much as moved. Baptiste and Loughlin set off for the door. After a few paces, Loughlin swung round.

'Seein' as we're here and, like I say, we're low on funds, maybe you'd best open that cash box you got there and make a donation.'

By the door Baptiste gave a low, rumbling laugh.

'Ain't nothin' here worth you fellows troublin' yourselves over, I ain't got . . .'

The gun came closer and Peebles shut up and pulled the metal box out from beneath the counter. It wasn't even locked. There were fifteen dollars in bills inside, a solitary gold one-dollar piece, three silver quarters, two dollars' worth of nickels and a bronze one-cent piece. Tap threw this back to Peebles, who caught it at the third attempt and held it foolishly in his open palm.

'You ain't about to try nothin' to stop us ridin' out of here?' asked Tap as he retreated towards the door.

Peebles shook his head, a few drops of sweat flicking away on either side. Why would he be so foolish as to do that when with any luck they'd ride out of the place none the wiser for missing the gold bars and silver coin that were inside a strongbox in the padlocked store room out back? Let them go!

'That's what I call being real sensible,' said Tap, feeling pretty pleased with himself.

Baptiste was already in the saddle, the boots dangling from the pommel and the parcel of clothes stuffed behind the saddle; he was fixing a length of rope about it as Loughlin came through the door.

'Easy enough,' shrugged Baptiste.

'Yeah,' said Tap. 'Why can't they all be that way?'

He mounted up, glanced back towards the place to make sure that the owner hadn't changed his mind.

'Let's go.'

The dog still lay in the centre of the street, flies buzzing now around the hole that had claimed just about half of its head. Blood congealed thickly and the dirt and dust were dark with it where it had run down. The man was still kneeling close by, oblivious of the fact that the corpse was setting up a fair stench. Maybe he stank so much himself he never would have noticed anyway.

'Jesus!' exclaimed Tap. 'Look at that!'

Baptiste shook his head. 'Poor bastard's left his senses.'

Tap nodded, averting his head as they came closer. 'Reckon so,' he agreed.

The two riders separated out, moving to pass man and dog on either side, giving them as wide a berth as possible. The man was murmuring to himself, words that made no sense as they drifted upwards, nothing more than a jumble of distraught thoughts. Baptiste cleared his throat and spat off to the front of the nearest shack.

As he did so, the dog's owner got to his feet and began to scream, a sudden violent invective against all the creatures of God's earth. Both Tap and Baptiste turned, startled by the man's ravings.

'Jesus!' exclaimed Tap again. 'Let's get the hell out of here.'

He swung out his legs to kick the horse into a little more pace and as he did so the man whirled both arms about his own head, shouting all the more. Loughlin's mount lurched off down the street and Baptiste sought to follow suit. As he turned his back and lashed out with his reins, the dog owner ceased to swirl his arms and brought them to a standstill in front of his body.

The Colt Navy was still tight in his hand.

Baptiste rocked in the saddle and the explosion roared through his head.

He arched steeply backwards, dropping the reins, clutching for something behind that he could never hope to reach.

The man dipped his head, cursed, and fired again. This time the slug grooved a path through the dirt of the street and finally embedded itself in a post twenty yards away to the side.

Baptiste could feel a deep stabbing pain in his back and his head was singing, a roaring, a ringing that seemed to dart back and forth between his ears. He could feel something warm trickling down the centre of his back, underneath the rough wool of his shirt.

Tap Loughlin kicked at his horse's flanks and drew the pistol from his belt. The horse shied under him and his finger came back jerkily against the trigger; the bullet soared off into the air. The man with the Colt Navy stood his ground, mouth open and a line of saliva drooling from one corner over his stubbled jaw. He saw Loughlin coming towards him and fired. Tap yelled disbelievingly as he felt something tug at his sleeve and the pistol was jolted from between his fingers.

He swung the horse wide again, once more having trouble controlling it. Baptiste was sitting hunched forward in his saddle, the pommel and the two pairs of boots pushed up against his stomach. His head still swam and his back was burning. His eyes kept flickering open but all the time he was aware that what they really wanted to do was stay shut.

The man in the middle of the street wasn't bothering with any more gunplay. As other folk appeared cautiously on the edges of the street, he realized what this pair were up to – they wanted his dog. He pushed the Colt Navy down into one of the capacious pockets of his old coat and, bending with some difficulty, he lifted the dead animal up into his arms.

Tap Loughlin stared at the sight of the man's haphazard progress, the legs of the animal pushing out on either side of his body as he ran. Tap cursed and looked at his arm, trying to figure out exactly how much damage the bullet had caused. All he could tell without tearing the sleeve completely away was that there wasn't a great deal of blood and the bone didn't seem to have been hit.

He glanced at his pistol, down in the dirt, at Baptiste's heavy body beginning to slide sideways from his saddle. Faces were staring at the two of them and down towards the end of the street – in the direction that the man and dog were heading – the bald head of Peebles was clear and unmistakable. He sure as hell didn't want to find himself stuck in the middle of a place turning all righteous and thinking it had itself a choice pair of outlaws to string up. He heard the word, 'penitentiary' and that was enough to make him realize that even here in Peebles' Halt, two and two weren't so hard to put together.

Tap dropped to his feet, called off a few curses as the pain jolted along his arm, and retrieved the pistol. He ran across to Baptiste and spoke to him urgently, propping him back up in the saddle and telling him to hold on till they put a little distance between themselves and the town. Holding the reins of Baptiste's mount in his left hand, he climbed back on to his own horse and got the two of them down that street and off back the way they'd come as fast as he was able.

Six

'What the hell are you runnin' here, Loughlin? I mean, what is this, some kind of joke outfit you set up for laughs? Let me call the shots, you said. I'm the one who knows what I'm doin'. It's me that knows what it's all about. Ain't I the feller who robs banks an' such for a livin'?' Majors stood tall in the middle of the group of men, pumping his fists out into the air, letting his voice swell and roar. He'd been drinking hard on the bottle of home-made liquor they'd taken from the farm house and there wasn't going to be any holding him. The only way to shut him up was going to be to knock him down – and out.

'Jesus, I should have known better than to have trusted some stumble-bum bandit who can't take a train without getting most of his gang either killed or wounded. Wholesale bloody carnage and at the end of it two of the bunch run off with the money and you haven't got a damned idea where they're gone. Jesus Christ! Loughlin, I'll tell you this – as an outlaw you're about as dangerous as a five-year-old kid with a stick of candy!'

Tap Loughlin glared up at Majors and then looked away at the embers around the edge of the fire. There were things he felt like saying, excuses he could make, but what would be the point? He'd feel even lower if he tried to apologize to a man like Majors, and the prospect of crawling in front of what was left of his outfit didn't suit him too well, either. With any luck, saying nothing was the best way to get Majors to shut his mouth.

There wasn't any such luck around.

Majors hauled the bottle from the ground, wiped his mouth around the neck to get the last drops and then hurled if off into the scrub. He got himself closer to Loughlin and pointed down at him with one of those ham-like hands.

'You know what you just did, don't you? You and your right-hand gun, over there. The one layin' groanin' with a slug in his back to go with the one he's already carryin' somewhere in that leg of his. You know what you done?'

Majors gave himself long enough pause to look quickly round

the rest to make sure they were giving him the attention he figured he deserved.

'You rode into this two-bit place an' stole a couple of suits of clothes and you couldn't even get away with that! You got yourselves shot up by who? The town marshal? Some tearaway punk provin' himself quick on the draw? Like hell you did! You got shot up by some lunatic hobo who'd just used the same gun to shoot his own dog. His dog!'

Majors' finger jerked close to Loughlin's shamed face.

'And then, an' this is the part that's real jim-dandy, you rode off with your tail between your legs, lettin' the feller go scot-free.'

'What would you have done?' Loughlin managed to get out, still not looking up.

'Me? I'd've taken that place apart and not before I'd put a couple of shots in that old fool's brain-pan the way he done to his dog.'

That's about it, Loughlin thought, shooting old men in the head and sticking knives in kids before you rape their sisters. That's your mark. He thought it but he didn't say it. He didn't say a thing.

'You ain't even got the guts to open your mouth, Loughlin. Jesus, you make me sick!'

Majors stepped back far enough to be able to clear his throat and hawk down a mouthful of phlegm that slid into the dirt inches away from Loughlin's boots.

It was enough to make Tap's back straighten and his hand move in the direction of his gun butt. Majors grinned and pushed back his coat, letting his own pistol show clear.

Neither of them moved near as fast as Gideon. The tall black seemed to be on his feet without anyone else realizing that he was moving. He set his large body between Majors and Loughlin and for once Lloyd Majors found himself having to look up.

'What's on your mind?' Majors growled.

'Just a thought.'

'Yeah?'

'That you could ease off on that mouth of yorn a little.'

Majors' eyes tightened, his mouth twitched; he wasn't used to being told what he could do and certainly not by some jumped-up nigger.

'Boy . . .' he began.

Gideon nearly laughed. 'Who do you think you're callin' *boy*?'

'While I got this gun here and you ain't,' said Majors, 'I'd say it was you.'

'Huh!' Gideon snorted and shook his head.

There was a movement from across the fire.

'My brother there, he ain't got no gun, but I sure have. You want to take a look, white boy?'

Majors gritted his teeth and flexed his fingers round the grip of his gun and looked. Joseph was sitting with one of the shotguns resting on his knee, and in the firelight his smile looked wide and handsome.

'I'd say,' said Joseph, 'that from this range I could spread your nice white gut all over forty yards of good ground. That is, if'n you want to take this matter a whole lot further.'

Joseph laughed and Gideon joined in with him, careful to step back out of range just in case his brother did let fly. He didn't want to be spread over no forty yards of ground, good or no.

'Way I see it,' Joseph went on, 'you been ridin' Tap over there till you're fit to bust. Like Gideon just said, wouldn't hurt none if you was to give your mouth a rest. After all,' Joseph laughed, 'anyone can get 'emselves shot in the back.'

Lloyd Majors licked his bottom lip; the muscles in his neck were straining fit to bust. He let his hand slide clear of his gun just the same. Joseph, saying nothing, nodded and set his shotgun on to the ground beside him.

'Okay,' Majors said after a while, 'we're still ridin' together till we get hold of some spendin' money. That agreed?'

He looked round the men once more; Levy and Little Kinney glanced at Loughlin and waited for him to say what he thought; as far as they were concerned it was still his show. Baptiste wasn't about to say anything. The pain that was driving down his spine gave him enough to concentrate on. Loughlin shrugged and sighed and grudgingly nodded.

'And this time,' Majors went on. 'I'm ridin' in first time. We don't want no more accidents.'

Joseph agreed that seemed fair enough. He and Gideon were having their own doubts about Loughlin as a leader, but the way they figured it, the sensible thing was to stick with him until the six thousand from the train was reached. After that, they'd go their own ways. As for Majors, they'd gladly have left him stretched out on the trail if it weren't for the fact that they needed him when they did hit a place with money worth taking.

Ozark was on the north bank of the Arkansas River. Ten years back it had been little more than a ferry crossing where the river looped north and the banks were slight enough to allow access. Now it was a pretty thriving place, far enough downriver from Fort Smith to stand on its own feet. Stores and smithys had sprung up to cater for the small farms and the ranches clustered around the fertile land of the river bottoms. Folk came in from south of the Mulberry and west of Piney Creek. Anyone who lived further north than that went to Cass, but that wasn't so many as to leave Ozark short of spenders.

The Arkansas Mercantile and Banking Company had opened a branch there four years back and the president, one Malcolm Grant, had come out himself to open the place up and see that the manager got the hang of things over the first few days. Steven Cash had worked as an assistant to Grant for several years at the head office in Fort Smith and most of that time he'd been biting back on his tongue and doing what he hoped were the right things to keep in the president's good books. Now he was his own boss as far as most things went and a life-time's ambition seemed to have come home to roost. With a name like his, what else could he have aspired to? His folks had joked about it when he'd set his mind on travelling west to make his living, carve a place for himself in the banking business. Now they weren't laughing, just pleased; more than pleased, according to the last letter he'd had. Delighted. Proud.

Cash had been pretty pleased when the new customer had come in that morning right as soon as Mrs Chowning had let up the shutters and rolled the green blind up from the glass door front, turning the *closed* sign so's it read *open*.

He was a mild-mannered man, not dressed all that well, but from the way he spoke, he'd bought a good spread to the south and had the money to stock it pretty good. He was making inquiries about the security of the bank for holding the cash he wanted to use on stock and Cash had shown him where the safe was kept and told him how thick it was and how secure the combination system was and things like that. The rancher had asked about guards and Cash had opened his jacket and showed him a deringer set into a nice leather shoulder holster that his wife, Laura, had bought him at the time of his promotion.

'That all?' the man had asked.

Cash had shook his head and pointed out the sawn-off shotgun fixed on pegs underneath the teller's counter.

'Know how to use it?' the man had joked with the teller.

Buddy Brayfield had blushed and said sure, all you had to do was get it pointed and pull the triggers, wasn't it?

The potential customer had looked impressed and said, well, yes, he guessed it was.

Cash had called Mrs Chowning over and asked her to give their new account holder a handout listing all of the bank's holdings and investments.

'Are you making a deposit this morning?' Mrs Chowning had asked with a smile. 'Mr, er . . .'

'Mr Danziger,' the manager informed her.

'Well, no, ma'am, not right now. But I'll be ridin' back this way real soon and I'll be sure to call in. I'm real impressed with the set-up here, I can tell you that.'

Mrs Chowning smiled and reddened up a little and glanced sideways at Mr Cash, thinking, as she often did, what a shame it was he was already married. And there so few eligible men around town for a young widow to be interested in.

'Good day, Mr Danziger,' called Cash as Tap Loughlin moved towards the door. Buddy Bradfield even came round from behind the grille to open the door. Loughlin gave him a friendly grin and stepped out on to the sidewalk.

His horse was tethered to the hitching rail outside the bank and the man standing gazing at it was around twenty-five years of age, wearing an off-white stetson with a deep crown and a look of suspicion on his clean-shaven face. Loughlin didn't notice the badge until he was closer still and he'd already made room for his hand to get at his pistol should it come necessary.

'Your horse?'

'Uh-huh.'

Loughlin began to unwind the reins from the rail, taking his time and not seeming at all rattled.

'Had her long?'

Loughlin shook his head. 'Couple of weeks, maybe. Bought her down south of here.'

The sheriff looked across the saddle. 'You got a bill of sale?'

'Sure.'

The sheriff held out his hand.

'Hold on now,' said Loughlin. 'I don't carry it with me. It's back at my place, though, if you want to see it.'

'What place is this?'

'Spread down by the Snake.'

'You just stake it out? I ain't seen you round here before.'

'Bought it,' Loughlin said, gripping the saddle pommel and keeping his right hand close to his gun.

The sheriff set his left hand up against the mare's bridle.

'Nothin' wrong, is there, Sheriff Dillon?' It was the bank manager, standing just outside his door, his face earnest and questioning.

''Lo, Mr Cash. Maybe not. Had a report of some stock stolen south of here a few days back, that's all.'

Cash came to the edge of the boardwalk, smiling his professional smile. 'Well, let me assure you, Mr Danziger here is not the kind of man who would knowingly purchase stolen stock. Mr Danziger's been visiting today to set up an account with the Arkansas Mercantile. He's on his way back to his place now that he's made sure our arrangements for security are satisfactory and he'll be riding back to town later to make a substantial deposit.' The smile widened. 'A substantial deposit.'

The sheriff let go of the bridle and stepped clear. 'In that case,' he said, 'Mr Danziger wouldn't mind bringin' that bill of sale in with him.'

Loughlin nodded and slipped his boot into the saddle. 'That's right, sheriff. I'll be sure to do exactly that.'

He set his fingers to the underside of his stetson. 'Good day, gentlemen.'

Sheriff and banker watched him as he rode down the main street, then turned to talk of the town social planned for the coming Saturday.

'There's a sheriff who looks a mite sharp,' said Loughlin, 'an' he'll take a little sittin' on. Scott, you can see to that. That apart, it's goin' to be easy enough. Damn bank manager's goin' to crawl so hard he's just about goin' to open the safe an' throw that money at us.'

'How much d'you reckon?' asked Little Kinney.

Loughlin shrugged. 'Anythin' between a thousand and three or four hundred.'

'That all?' exclaimed Majors.

'It's enough,' said Joseph. 'For now.'

'Split six ways,' said Majors.

Loughlin shook his head. 'Seven.'

Majors whirled round and pointed at where Baptiste was stretched out in a blanket. 'He ain't ridin' with us, he don't get no share-out.'

'Majors, I told you to keep your mouth out of business as don't concern you.'

'Well, this does. You want me to risk my neck on account of some lame-brain who gets hisself shot up by a fool old man.'

Loughlin stared hard. 'You don't want to risk your neck, stay out.'

Majors thought for a moment, then threw back his head in a mighty laugh. 'That'd suit you fine, wouldn't it? So's you could ditch me here without a damned thing. I'm comin' in.'

Loughlin pointed down at Baptiste. 'And he gets his cut.'

Majors shrugged. 'Okay.'

'Besides,' said Loughlin, going down on to his haunches, 'Baptiste ain't the only one not goin' into Ozark.'

'What's your idea, Tap?' asked Levy.

Loughlin waited until he had everyone's attention. 'We ride in heavy-handed, there's goin' to be trouble. They'll spot somethin' right off. Sheriff ain't got no more to do as it is than check every horse brand that rides through town.

'Scott, you an' Gideon there ride down a couple of hours before the rest of us. You take Baptiste with you. He can ride if'n you don't have to travel too fast. The two of you carry on through and wait for us maybe an hour's journey up the north trail. Gideon, you hang back in case there's any trouble gettin' out. Stay where you can use a rifle to snap off any damn posse as might be tailin'. You got that?'

They had. Tap coughed, cleared his throat and went on.

'Kinney, you get into Ozark an hour after them. Take a look around. You see anythin' unusual like a convention of marshals suddenly hit town, ride back out nice an' easy and tell us. We'll skirt Ozark and meet up on the other side. Otherwise, you just get yourself a couple of beers and sit out on the sidewalk, watch the day go by. I'm ridin' in with Joseph and we'll head straight for the bank, banker's expectin' me so that's fine. He'll have a red carpet out on the steps when he sees me headin' in. Joseph, you stay outside with the horses, keep your eyes skinned up and down that street.'

Tap looked at last at Majors.

'I want you followin' us into town. No more'n half a mile behind. You want to be in on this, you're goin' to be. I'll stall around inside the bank, passin' the time of day real pleasant, until you walk in. Then we just stick 'em up and take 'em for all they got.'

He rubbed his hands, one palm across the other. Pointed to the bottle over by Little Kinney, who passed it over. Loughlin wiped his sleeve carelessly across the lip and drank.

'How 'bout this sheriff?' asked Majors.

'Scared?' taunted Loughlin.

'He's got a fair question,' Levy pointed out.

'Okay. What we do is this. That lawman steps out of his office, appears anywhere along the street while we're in the bank, Kinney takes him out.'

'Just gun him down?' asked Little Kinney, his uneven-coloured eyes uncertain.

'Hell, you can go over an' talk to him, distract him till you get the drop on him. Get his gun and hammer him over the head with it. I don't give a damn. Just stop him interferin'.'

'And if he don't show till we're on the way out of town?' asked Joseph.

Loughlin smiled quietly. 'Then he's fair game for anyone.' He stood up. 'Any more questions?'

Everyone shook their heads. It sounded easy as sneakin' coffee cake off your maid-aunt's kitchen shelf without gettin' whipped for it. Even Lloyd Majors had to admit – though never out loud – that for once it sounded as though Loughlin knew what the hell he was talking about. Come to think of it, he had got them out of that damned pen pretty good, too. And then there was this railroad money that they'd been whisperin' about amongst themselves, thinkin' that he didn't know what was going on. Majors snorted to himself: maybe it'd pay him to stick around with Tap Loughlin longer than either of them had figured.

Seven

Little Kinney, as you might imagine, wasn't called that on account of his being small. Neither was he particularly big. Certainly he wasn't either as tall or as broad as Baptiste and when it came to the two blacks who were now riding with them, well, he didn't come close. No, the thing was he'd been born with a twin brother, the pair of them difficult to distinguish except for their sizes and Little Kinney's mixed-up eyes, one blue and the other bright enough green. So when they got old enough not to be crawling around on all fours, Kinney's brother was called Big Kinney and he was Little Kinney. Had been ever since. It didn't matter that his twin brother wasn't around any more. Hadn't been since he'd trod on a rattler down near the Texas border.

Little Kinney settled in the rickety wooden chair, one of four that was pushed up against the wall out front of the saloon. Since the boards of the sidewalk were pretty uneven it wasn't the easiest of tasks to get balanced. But he did and pretty soon he was enjoying the shade from the sun afforded by the saloon's balcony and the beer, which wasn't halfway bad. He stretched his legs and yawned a little and thought that he could get used to a life doing nothing much more than this.

He was close to the bottom of his beer and considering whether it was worth disturbing his own comfort to fetch another, when the sheriff appeared in the corner of his vision. Little Kinney held his breath, teeth knocking against the rim of the glass. Under the lowered brim of his brown, sweat-stained hat, out of this green eye, he could see the lawman walking slow and easy up the street, leading a horse. Kinney carefully adjusted himself so that he could see with both eyes. The animal was a high-stepping bay, and from the state of its coat it had that minute come from the livery stable where it had been curried and combed. The sheriff was looking pretty damn spruce, too. Clean-shaven and his shirt white and uncreased, even a little starch around the collar. His pants were thick denim and his gun belt shone more than the bay's mane when it took the sun. The off-white stetson was pinched deep at the crown; the badge on the fresh shirt shone not a little itself.

Little Kinney wondered just how good he was, prancing up the high street looking like something out of a rodeo at county fair. He didn't figure a lawman who was any damn good for real would show himself off that way.

Least, he hoped that to be the case.

He stayed where he was, boot heels hooked round the rung of the chair, while the sheriff walked slowly past. Sheriff Dillon gave him no more than a glance, and that was all Kinney would have expected. He wasn't any kind of an exceptional man to look at. Finally, the lawman tied up his horse outside the building advertising itself as the sheriff's office and town jail and, with a final look both ways along the street, went inside out of the sun.

Little Kinney waited a few minutes and then lowered the chair down on to all four legs and got himself another beer.

Tap Loughlin was wearing a cream alpaca coat he'd taken from the farm they'd robbed after breaking out of the penitentiary. His pistol was tucked down into his belt; he never had liked wearing a proper holster much and never usually did. Baptiste had told him some story about a feller who carried a .45 like that and shot his balls off one day reaching fast for his gun. As a yarn it hadn't done a lot for Tap's stomach, but he didn't see that he was going to be so foolish. He didn't see himself as any kind of quick-draw specialist anyhow. Simply liked the butt of his weapon close to hand. Where it was now.

He glanced over at Joseph and was glad that the two Negroes had thrown in with him and the rest of the bunch. They were strong and didn't seem to mind taking orders, either. God knows, they needed replacements and plenty after that fool business at the train.

Jesus damn!

He pushed back his hat and wiped his arm across under the brim.

'Hot, ain't it?' grinned Joseph, his face wet with sweat.

Loughlin nodded. 'Sure is.'

But he was still running his mind over the debacle of the train. The one thing that didn't occur to him was that it was in any way Sara-Lee's fault. She'd been the one who'd put him up to it, persuaded him that it would be a better thing than all those little banks they'd been robbing, and eventually he'd gone along. Her insistence had pushed him into it, but that didn't matter. He should have got it right, had got it right, but for those damned railroad people sneaking extra men in there and then blasting all hell out of his bunch without giving them a chance.

It weren't right.

Weren't right that he hadn't seen Sara for so long either.

She came back to him now as he rode down towards the ferry that would carry Joseph and himself across the Arkansas and into Ozark. Hair dark as a raven's wing and spectacles she wore from all that reading – and when she took them off and the light caught the dark brown of her eyes!

'Ferry's over here an' waitin',' called Joseph.

'Yeah,' mumbled Tap, as if from a dream. 'Yeah, sure. Okay.'

When they grounded on the north bank of the river, the substantial figure of Lloyd Majors was waiting back on the bottom shore. Everything was going according to plan; like it had the time they were taking the bank money from the AT&SF. Only that thought didn't occur to Loughlin. There was nothing, as he rode along the broad main street, to trouble his mind.

Joseph was half a length behind him. There were few others around. An old timer sitting on the left-hand side of the street, Little Kinney instantly recognizable to Loughlin down opposite, his chair leaning back against the saloon wall. Out front of the sheriff's office there was a handsome looking bay. A mule-drawn high-sided wagon was coming down in the other direction, a one-armed man holding the reins, a skinny kid of around eleven or twelve up there beside him.

Tap nodded down at Little Kinney, much as any traveller might do, no more than passing the time of day.

Kinney mumbled something by way of reply and lifted his half-empty glass in salute.

Joseph looked through the window at the front of the sheriff's office to see if he could catch a glimpse of the man, but there was nothing. The sign outside the bank was bright and looked freshly repainted. ARKANSAS MERCANTILE AND BANKING COMPANY. This time there was a face at the window and it jutted forward then pulled away as Loughlin and Joseph approached. By the time Tap had slid from the saddle, Steven Cash was standing in the open doorway, smile set on his face and his right hand extended in welcome.

Tap handed his reins up to Joseph and stepped on to the boardwalk. As he shook the bank manager's hand, he glimpsed Majors at the far end of the street. Tap frowned: he was pushing it awful damn close.

'Anything wrong?' asked Cash.

'Huh? No. No, nothin'. Just a thought is all.'

'That's fine. Won't you step inside?'

Buddy Brayfield beamed out from behind his teller's position, his freckles strong enough to show clearly through the wire grille. Mrs Chowning gave a smile from her desk back of the counter and revised her opinion of the new account holder – he was almost as handsome as Mr Cash himself. A few years older, maybe, and his nose wasn't altogether straight on his face, but he had a generous mouth and, above all, honest eyes. Yes, that was a telling factor, honest eyes.

'I've had the necessary papers made out, Mr Danziger. If you'd care to step through and into my office we could get the formalities over in just a few moments.'

The office was to the right, its door facing Mrs Chowning's desk. Cash left the door open and set the papers down in front of Loughlin.

'You brought your deposit, I see,' said the bank manager, nodding at the bulge beneath the buttoned alpaca coat.

'Oh, yeah.'

'Money belt, I suppose?'

'That's right.'

Loughlin shifted his position so that he had a good view of the woman and could see one side of the bank teller, nothing, though of the door. That didn't matter, he'd be sure to hear Majors enter.

Cash was dangling a pen before Loughlin's face. 'If you'd like to put your signature here . . . and here . . . and one more time, here.'

Tap grinned good-humouredly. 'That's a whole mess of names, ain't it?'

Out in the main section of the bank, Buddy Brayfield had begun to whistle.

Cash was still holding out the pen, still smiling. Loughlin pointed down at the papers. 'Three times, huh?'

'That's right, Mr Danziger. Just three times.'

The door to the bank was hurled open loud and fast and Brayfield's tune ended in a surprised splutter. Majors' voice boomed: 'Don't nobody move!' Tap Loughlin drew in the sides of his mouth and reached inside his alpaca coat. Staring, not wanting to believe, Steven Cash watched as the pistol slid up from Loughlin's belt.

'Danziger!' the bank manager gasped.

'Uh-uh, friend,' said Loughlin softly, 'you got the name wrong. Now while everyone else is kind of busy outside, would you mind opening up that safe of yours?'

Cash's eyes were blinking fast and all of the colour had drained from his face.

Lloyd Majors had got to the end of the counter, a hinged flap of wood that he rammed back hard. Buddy Brayfield winced at the crack and Mrs Chowning pressed her hands down over her ears. Majors glanced at her quickly and then looked a second time, more carefully. The way her hands were raised pulled the silky material of her dress awful tight across her breasts.

Something was ticking away inside Brayfield's brain, some fool idea that he couldn't shake. His hands were trembling and his left foot was tapping a quiet, insistent tattoo on the boards.

'You got a nice big sack there, sonny?'

Buddy nodded.

'Okay. Then scoop all you got out from under that counter and fill her up.'

The tick wouldn't go away; his hands wouldn't stop shaking. Buddy looked quickly over at Mrs Chowning, but her eyes were closed tight as if she was waiting for some fierce onset of pain.

'Now, sonny!'

Buddy Brayfield turned sideways to Majors, facing the counter. He stretched over a little to his right and began to pull out the drawers, exposing bills and coins set in neat columns. Majors beamed. Buddy got as far as the third drawer and then his hands knocked against the sawn-off barrels of the shotgun. A pulse raced at his temple. He jerked the gun clear of its pegs, his thumbs bumped clumsily against the hammers, feeling swollen. Majors was staring at the woman's chest. Buddy spun round and swung the shotgun towards the big man who bulked at the end of the counter.

Majors flattened himself against the side wall and fired twice.

The sound of his pistol was lost in the roar of the shotgun.

Mrs Chowning screamed, certain that she had been shot. Her hands dragged away from her ears and clasped her breasts.

Chunks of plaster and lathe flew across the room.

Buddy Brayfield was hurled back against the counter, his body turning, his neat, well-pressed suit already darkening with blood. The brown freckles that covered his nose and cheeks were spotted red. The pulse that pushed haphazardly against his tight skin beat with less and less force. He slumped at the knees, arms grabbing sideways; one of the money drawers came toppling towards him. Nickels and dimes bounced and rolled. Crisp banknotes fluttered into the air.

Inside his office, Cash was leaning hard against the side of the safe, mouth open and fighting for breath. His eyes were no longer blinking, were wide. He was looking at Loughlin, looking at the gun which had swung away towards the door at the sound of firing from outside. Cash was thinking about the president of the bank, about the trust that Grant had imposed upon him. He read the indecision in Loughlin's face and made a grab for the gun. Loughlin reacted, but not quickly enough. The two men staggered several yards sideways and collided with a glass-fronted cabinet set against the wall. Plate glass cracked and crashed and the shelves spilled their contents on to the floor. Both of Cash's hands were tight round Loughlin's wrist, trying to force the pistol from his fingers.

Loughlin swung his left arm and brought his fist down into the side of the bank manager's head. Cash grunted and his head moved painfully, but he didn't relinquish his grip. Loughlin punched him again and again and the two of them swayed and lurched around the office, rebounding from desk to wall and back again.

The gun was raised high above both their heads and Loughlin's finger pressed back on the trigger hard enough to release a bullet into the ceiling.

Mrs Chowning leapt up from her desk and began to run around the space behind the counter, her hands still clapped to her ears and her mouth open to a succession of shrill screams.

Majors, down on one knee scooping money into a large white sack, raised his pistol and shot her through the side.

The woman went into the doorway of Cash's office as if she'd been kicked. Her shoulder hit the door jamb and she slowly slid down the wall towards the floor. Blood was leaking through her ribs, through the smooth material of her dress, clouding its silky shine. Her right hand moved to the wound and found the stickiness of the blood. The other hand covered her mouth but she could still hear her own screams.

Loughlin brought his knee up into the bank manager's groin and thudded the underneath of his elbow crisp against his chin. Cash's teeth rammed together and he bit off a quarter-inch of his tongue. He let go of Loughlin's right wrist and Tap swung the pistol free and drove its barrel end sideways across Cash's face. The sight grooved a deep line through the flesh of his cheek and he tumbled, half-conscious, to the ground.

As Loughlin began to feel in his pockets for the keys to the safe, he heard the sound of shooting from the street.

His fingers froze on the steel ring.

Through the open doorway he caught Majors' gaze, the scorn, the eyes that said I told you.

Little Kinney had been standing close by his horse; he had seen Majors enter the bank in the wake of Tap Loughlin and he knew that at any moment they'd be riding out of Ozark as if there was a bunch of vigilantes on their tail. He saw the black astride his horse outside the bank and saw that he was holding the reins of the other two mounts. Everything seemed to be going off just like Tap had planned it. Even the sheriff hadn't shown himself outside his office; the door had shut behind him and stayed shut.

Kinney licked his lips, dry still after two glasses of beer. He turned the leather of the reins over his hand and pushed his left boot into the stirrup. What he wasn't prepared for was the blast of the shotgun that echoed out from the bank.

Kinney's skin froze up along the back of his neck; his stomach tightened like an old maid's fist and his whole mouth was dry now. He wiped his hand across his lips and turned towards the opposite side of the street. He was watching the door and the door of the sheriff's office wasn't opening.

Little Kinney still had his foot slotted into the stirrup.

He still had his foot slotted into the stirrup when Sheriff John Dillon shot him.

The lawman had left the building through the rear door and come quiet around the side. He'd seen Kinney watching the front and that had been enough. His Colt had come up smooth, the hammer had clicked quietly back and he'd sighted along the top of the barrel, arm bent. The .45 slug ripped through the back of Kinney's left arm and dug into his back above the shoulder blade. It tore away a good deal of flesh and span away into the front of the saloon, where it embedded itself in the wall.

Little Kinney tried to turn and face the sheriff, but his foot was trapped in the stirrup and as he twisted, his leg got hoisted up and he fell, head-first, to the ground.

That was how come Dillon's second shot sailed a couple of feet above his body and whined away off the saloon doors.

Another shot rang out from the bank and Dillon hesitated, not certain whether Kinney was going to be coming back up or not.

He figured that if he did, he wouldn't cause too many problems. The bank was more important. He cut back on to the sidewalk and started to run, his boots loud on the loose, echoing boards. Joseph saw him coming and yelled a warning to those inside. He freed the rifle from under the flap of the saddle and brought it up against his shoulder.

Dillon was still running.

Joseph's first shot tore away a chunk of the wooden pillar holding up the upper storey of the general store; his second smashed the glass of the store window to smithereens. Dillon raised his left arm to protect his face from the shards of flying glass and dropped to one knee. He steadied his right hand with his left tight at its wrist. The .45 roared once and Joseph felt the wind of the slug as it whipped past him and ricocheted off the front of the bank.

There were men running now, up and down the street, some of them carrying arms, but none so far interested in getting involved in the shooting. Dillon called out orders, waving his hands wildly. If anyone understood, they didn't show any signs of obeying.

'Bastards!' Dillon yelled. Whose money did they think he was trying to protect anyway?

Joseph was out of the saddle now and up by the bank door, pushing it open and shouting inside. He saw the sheriff run another fifteen yards before taking aim again with his pistol. Joseph just got on the far side of the door in time.

Majors was hurrying across from the counter, a sack bouncing up and down on his shoulder. Tap Loughlin had stopped fiddling with the safe keys and gone through the drawers of the manager's desk instead. Papers, papers and more papers. Cash started to come round and Loughlin looked at him with quick and real hatred and brought back his right leg. He planted the underside of his boot full in Cash's face and broke his nose.

'Let's go!' yelled Majors, almost knocking Joseph over in his hurry to get through the door.

The horses were moving free in the street, hooves ploughing up the dirt and dust.

'Jesus!' exclaimed Majors. 'The horses!'

Joseph ignored him and ducked low, making a dash for the nearest mount. A couple of shots rang out and it looked as if at least one of the townsfolk was helping the lawman now.

Down the street, Little Kinney had managed to push himself into a crouching position and had wiped the dirt from his eyes and mouth. He started to get up and someone hit him in the small of the back with a length of timber. Kinney cursed and fell sideways, rolling over, wincing with the sharp pain that shot through him again and again. He saw a man advancing on him, the piece of wood swinging above his head. Kinney reached for his pistol and his fingers closed round air; the holster was empty. The timber swung for his head and at the last moment Kinney ducked underneath it. He grabbed for the man's arm and caught hold; pulled him off-balance and scrambled to his feet himself. As the man stirred on the street, Kinney kneed him in the side of the head. He saw his gun in the dirt and bent to retrieve it. A badly aimed shot tried for him and missed by several feet. Kinney turned his horse around and hauled himself with difficulty into the saddle.

He saw the sheriff down on one knee to the left of the bank, using a water trough for cover while he reloaded his Colt. There seemed to be a couple of others putting in their two cents' worth – one back of some barrels over by the right and another at a first floor window.

Kinney let out a holler and kicked the horse's flanks hard. Flicking the reins over, side to side, he galloped down towards the bank, firing as he went. More by luck than anything else one of his shots went close enough to the sheriff to tear the heel off his right boot. Dillon dropped a handful of cartridges from his fingers and flattened himself behind the trough.

By this time Tap Loughlin had emerged from the bank and seen the only free horse disappearing down the street at a steady lick. A man at an upstairs window opposite knocked the glass clear and drew a bead on Loughlin as he hesitated in the doorway.

'Tap! Here!'

Loughlin moved in response to Kinney's call and a slug split the now vacant doorway in two. Majors fired a couple of times at the man back of the barrels and kept him from joining in any further, frightening rather than hitting him.

The sheriff had loaded his Colt and was about to take a hand in the play once again. A group of men were advancing from the direction of the saloon, looking as if they meant business.

'Joseph, let's move!'

Tap climbed up behind Kinney and gave the horse a whack on the rump. Majors was already charging away towards the northern edge of town, the sack of money bouncing out from the side of the horse as he went. Joseph was fifty yards behind him and another thirty yards back Kinney and Tap made themselves as small a target as they could.

Sheriff Dillon was torn between trying to shoot them down and calling together a posse to give chase.

There was an ominous silence from inside the bank.

Breathing hard, Tap Loughlin rode with one arm tight round Little Kinney's waist, the blood that was steadily oozing from Kinney's back already beginning to stick to his shirt and the lapels of his alpaca jacket.

Eight

The thicket lay between two ranges of hills pushing up north of Ozark towards the Mulberry River. The posse had been shaken off with ease, none of the riders apart from the sheriff overkeen on charging in upon an ambush, not one of them who didn't prefer to spend that night back at home in front of his own fire, eating his own food. So, hampered as they were by two badly wounded men, Tap Loughlin's bunch had been able to ride fast enough and far enough to shake off any fear of immediate pursuit. Even to light a fire.

The smoke drifted lazily upwards through the surrounding dogwood and green ash, smelling sweet and dry. A pan of boiling water simmered next to a smaller pan of warmed-over coffee grounds. Loughlin and Scott Levy were doing their best to clean up the pair of wounded men. Little Kinney's back was grooved through pretty deeply and the flesh on either side of the bullet's path had swollen up and was a passing imitation of deep purple. Baptiste's scabs had broken open during the ride and now the pieces of hard, brittle surface were interwoven with bright yellow puss and congealing blood.

'What the hell is it about your men that they only get shot in the back?' asked Majors, standing at the opposite side of the fire to Loughlin.

Tap caught his breath, caught his temper, let the remark ride. There wasn't a whole lot he could do about Majors working off his mouth and there were a whole lot of things more important right then. He was conscious enough of the mess they were in; knew that the second attempt to take a place for its money had gone badly wrong. The sack had contained a little over two hundred dollars and that was already shared out between the seven of them. It wasn't near as much as he planned for, not enough to get them very far. He knew only too well that the bank raid had been a disaster and that if it hadn't been for Little Kinney coming in like hell itself to pull him out, he would have been dead on that street within minutes. Dead and not a dollar in his pockets to show for it.

But Majors wasn't about to let it slide so easy. He pushed the toe of his boot into the edge of the fire, dislodging a batch of twigs and making the flames blaze up bright enough to show the anger in his eyes.

'I guess it couldn't be somethin' to do with bein' yeller, could it?' taunted Majors.

Tap's hand squeezed down on the piece of bloodied cloth with which he'd been swabbing Little Kinney's back and watery red trickled down into his palm and along his wrist, down through his fingers.

Scott Levy thought about reaching for the pistol at his belt, but then a fresh glance at Majors told him it wouldn't be the wisest thing to do. Better to wait and see the way things broke – after all, Tap hadn't been running things so well lately. He'd been saying the same to Gideon earlier and the big black had nodded his head and agreed.

'Could be they take after you,' Majors continued. 'Yeller like the man they run with.'

Tap threw down the cloth and whirled round; there was anger enough in his own face and his fists were bunched tight. His weapon, though, was lying on top of the alpaca coat, more feet away from his reach than it should have been at that moment. Majors looked big and powerful and his head jutted forward towards Loughlin as he spoke.

'Hear what I'm callin' you, Loughlin? Yeller!'

The words half-choked on Tap's lips. 'I hear you.'

'And?'

'And there's men enough here who'll say it ain't so.' Tap's eyes flicked round the edges of the fire, wondering not so much how many men would support him with words, but how many he could count on if it came to a fight. Baptiste and Little Kinney were the only ones he could have relied upon whatever the argument, whatever the situation – and they were shot up pretty bad and face down on blankets with their wounds half-dressed. Levy he was less and less sure of. There was something he only registered now, the way Scott had avoided his eyes the last day or so, saying nothing more than he had to. Tap wondered now, too late, how much talk Scott Levy had been having with Majors on the quiet.

As for the blacks, Tap had no idea. They'd showed support for him against Majors once before, but that had been the other side of Ozark and how much longer were they going to carry on backing a losing hand?

Majors grinned. 'I'm listening hard, Loughlin, but I can't hear anyone sayin' overmuch.'

Tap shrugged, shifted his feet; if only that pistol of his weren't so far off. Majors' own gun was only inches from his hand and he was only looking for the chance to use it. They both knew that: all the men round the fire knew it. It was for Loughlin to decide – either he was yeller the way Majors had said and he'd accept it and lose face, lose control of the gang – or he could make a dive for his gun and get shot for certain.

Tap's throat was dry but his hands were damp with sweat. The sweet smell of woodsmoke choked his nostrils.

'What's it to be, Loughlin?' sneered Majors.

Tap kicked at the loose earth before the fire. 'You think what you damn well like!'

He said it with as much force as he could but could tell straight off that it didn't carry a lot of weight with those who were still making up their minds, with Gideon and Joseph, maybe Levy. He heard one of the blacks snort with disgust and saw Scott Levy turn away as if he were embarrassed.

Loughlin turned away himself, going back to his knees and taking up the piece of cloth with which he'd been wiping Little Kinney's back. He shook it free of dirt and then plunged it into the boiling water before reapplying it to the wound.

Majors stood at the centre of things for a while longer but he didn't need to say anything else and neither did anyone else. It was over: decided. At sun-up, they rode out, taking the bulk of the supplies with them – Majors, Gideon and Joseph, a somewhat shamefaced Scott Levy. Loughlin would have shaken him by the hand, wished him well, but Levy was too ashamed even to look him in the eye.

Not a word was spoken: nothing. Just the sound of horses moving off through the thicket and after that an occasional sound and the sight of four riders moving through the tree line as they trailed the side of the hill up to the Mulberry.

The remaining three said little enough; there didn't seem to be a whole lot to talk about. Not that that was going to make their row seem any easier to hoe. They had around sixty dollars between them, which would keep them in food and supplies and buy some fresh ammunition. But it wasn't going to last them very long if they ran into difficulties. Loughlin and Little Kinney had pistols and Baptiste still had one of the shotguns they had taken from the State Penitentiary. Baptiste was as strong as a mule. He ground his teeth hard together and pulled himself slowly up into the saddle. The gunshot wound in his back pained him worst, but since that had happened the pair of wounds he'd taken in his leg at the train had started playing up a lot more than the previous few days. Still, he had the physical strength to cope. His dark eyes were as bright as ever; his expression as determined. The thick beard and moustache hid from view the slight grimacing of the mouth whenever one or other pain jolted through his body.

Little Kinney took his troubles less quietly. Alternately cursing the sheriff for shooting him in the back and cursing Majors for leaving them like he had, Kinney's face was permanently screwed up with this or another anger. Neither was he as naturally strong as Baptiste; when his wound troubled him he wasn't powerful enough to shake it off, pretend that it wasn't happening. Instead, he doubled forward with the pain, moaning and lashing out into the air with his hands.

'You know where they're goin' to be headin', don't you?' said Baptiste when they were a half mile along the trail.

Tap Loughlin nodded. 'Right enough.'

'You know that bastard Levy's goin' to lead 'em right to it.'

Tap shook his head. 'Not right to it, he ain't. He don't know exactly where that railroad money is no more'n we do. Hell, it could be halfway across the entire damn country from here f'r all we know.'

Baptiste looked round. A small brown-winged bird moved between the upper branches of an ash. 'But he's goin' to lead Majors up across the border. He's settin' him on the trail sure enough.'

Little Kinney cursed and whistled. Cursed some more. 'Six thousand dollars!'

'Yeah!' hissed Baptiste and spat down to the ground.

Tap shook the reins and moved the horse into a trot. 'They ain't got it yet,' he said. 'Not yet they ain't.'

A few hundred yards on, he slowed again, realizing that neither of the men with him was going to push his mount above a walk unless it was unavoidable. The journey was going to take days longer than necessary under normal circumstances – unless he could get them patched up real good and able to ride properly. Or unless he left them to their own devices and went on alone.

Tap turned in the saddle and gazed back down the trail and all he could see was Little Kinney galloping along that main street in Ozark and hollering his name.

No: he wouldn't be riding on ahead. Not yet awhile.

They were climbing a steep slope towards the summit and a short cut to the river when Little Kinney lost his balance and tumbled sideways from the saddle. This time his foot jerked free of the stirrup right enough and all he suffered was a hefty thump on his arm and ribs and part of his back. But it was sufficient to open up the wound again and they had to wait while the bandages were removed and replaced. Loughlin could see them falling further and further behind, he could see Majors getting on the track of the money, he could see . . .

He stood upright and what he saw chilled him. It was Sara-Lee opening the door to the cabin where she lived in Springfield and there in the doorway bulked Lloyd Majors, blocking out the light.

Tap closed his eyes and his fingers went for a moment to the side of his head.

'You okay?'

Tap blinked at Baptiste and nodded slowly. 'Yeah,' he said in a flat tone. 'I'm fine.'

But all the time now he was conscious of how much they were holding him back, of how much more urgent catching up with Majors was likely to be.

'What's that up the road?'

Tap Loughlin reined in and followed the direction of Baptiste's outflung arm.

It was a high-sided, canvas-sailed wagon travelling slower than they were, but in the same direction. There was some coloured smudging on the sides, lettering maybe, but from that distance it wasn't possible to make it out clearly.

'Some kind of trader?' Tap offered.

'We could use some more shells,' said Little Kinney.

'Some jerky,' suggested Baptiste.

But the wagon turned out to have more for them than shells and beef jerky. Seymore Hardcastle was taking a rest from driving the pair of mules; his afternoon siesta, as he liked to call it. A couple of shots of his own cure-all and he laid down on the mattress in the back of the wagon and it never took him more than five or ten minutes to be fast asleep. Truth was, it never took Seymore more than that long to fall asleep anytime, anywhere. Myra was handling the reins, mouthing off at the mules for their stubbornness under her breath and now and again throwing small stones at their rumps. Neither the curses nor the stones made the least bit of difference and Myra would have lost her temper and hollered loud if she hadn't have known it would have waked the baby. Not Seymore, no fear of that, just the baby. So she tolerated the mules grudgingly, thankful of the peace she was enjoying while the child slept.

As it was, she was soon disturbed by the sound of horses and, looking around the side of the wagon, she saw it was three men coming up behind. The fact that they were in no apparent hurry made their appearance less threatening, though not such that she didn't check the load in her .38 Remington and stash it under the folds of her dress, real close to where she'd lay her right hand.

'Ma'am.'

Myra turned and nodded, taking in the speaker quickly, the one who'd drawn off from his companions. Stubble-faced, an alpaca coat and no gun belt but that didn't mean he didn't have a pistol stashed somewhere.

She looked into Tap Loughlin's face and made one of her instant judgements: she thought he might be all right. The pair riding with him, though – something strange about the way they held themselves in the saddle and that big bearded feller looked mean as she guessed a grizzly would be if ever she came across one face to face.

'Saw your sign there,' Tap pointed at the wagon's lettering, the words CURE-ALL suggesting that they might have come across exactly what they wanted.

'You a doctor?' Tap asked, turning his horse sideways on to the wagon.

'Me?' Myra laughed and her breasts shook loosely inside the top of her dress. She saw Loughlin following their movement and she wasn't displeased. 'No, I ain't no doctor. Why you askin'? You sick?'

'Not me.' Tap nodded towards Baptiste and Little Kinney.

'Them?'

'Uh-huh. Run into a scrape a ways back. Took a little gunshot.'

Myra nodded, looking at Loughlin afresh, resting her fingers on the butt of the .38 beneath her dress, hard and reassuring under the softness of the material.

'Cure-all ain't goin' to do nothing for gunshot wounds,' she said, after a while.

'Might be some bandages in that wagon. Might be you could help if you was willin'. I tried dressing 'em myself but my hands just don't sit right, doin' a job like that.'

Myra looked at him still, half in her mind to ask: what kind of a job do them hands of yours sit right doing?

But she held her tongue and nodded towards the rear of the wagon. 'Mr Hardcastle back there, if he was awake, he might do something for your friends.'

Tap Loughlin looked at the wagon a shade anxiously. Then he patted his coat pocket and Myra heard coins rattle together. 'You suppose that sound might wake him up?'

Myra almost smiled. 'It might.'

The baby stirred and she turned her head towards the child, hushing and shushing softly. As she did this the shaggy head of Seymore Hardcastle appeared through the canvas at the back of the seat. The man blinked several times, adjusting to the light; looked seriously and long at Loughlin and the men with him; reached back into the wagon and brought out his broken-down top hat, which he jammed fast on to his balding head.

'I believe certain of you gentlemen are in need of medical assistance,' he said.

The wagon was pulled off the trail and into the shade. There was an argument, not very prolonged, about the precise fee to be paid for Hardcastle's services. Then Baptiste and Little Kinney were helped up into the wagon and laid down side by side on the mattress, while Myra boiled water on the fire she and Tap had built close by. Seymore Hardcastle found a giant-size bottle of cure-all which he used to disinfect his own hands in the proper surgical manner; that done, Hardcastle rinsed a small, sharp knife in the same liquid and promptly splashed more over the patients' backs. Both Baptiste and Kinney hollered, Little Kinney in particular, but Hardcastle assured them that all they'd experienced was a good sign that the cure-all was doing its job. 'After all,' he said, 'you don't want nothin' gangrenous settin' in there, do we?' He rubbed his hands together, laughed, and began to probe around.

Tap Loughlin persuaded Myra that some of the boiling water wouldn't come amiss being put to some coffee grounds, and they sat, trying not to listen to what was happening under canvas, passing the time of day as pleasant as they could.

Tap was thinking how Myra, with her mess of brown hair and her ample figure – not to mention the child she was cuddling to her breast – wasn't exactly the kind of woman he'd like to have dreams about. She wasn't no Sara-Lee Danziger and that was certain. But there was a warmth and a frankness about her that made him feel, well, more attracted than he felt comfortable being.

For her part, Myra was pretty positive that Tap was one of the better looking strangers she'd come across in the past month or so. Nice enough, in fact, for her to wish that she could give her baby over to someone else for a time and wander off into the nearest clump of trees with him.

She even considered handing the child into Seymore, but then he sounded to have his hands full enough as it was. And, besides, how could she be sure he was interested – the stranger? Huh! Myra smiled to herself. What man wasn't, when it came down to it? None that she'd ever met. No, the way he was cradling that coffee mug in his hands and looking at her body, she was certain enough.

Myra eased herself a little closer and Tap did nothing to shift away.

'Myra!' Hardcastle's voice called out from the interior of the wagon. 'Myra! Get in here and help me bind these two up good and fast.'

She sighed and gave Tap the baby to hold instead.

Fifteen minutes later, all four were standing talking, drinking a final mug of coffee before the three riders set off on their way again. Little Kinney and Baptiste felt like trussed chickens, but now their wounds had been properly cleaned and bound and weren't likely to come open again at the first jolt in the journey.

'Travellin' far?' asked Hardcastle.

'Up Missouri way,' said Tap quickly, owing them a civil answer, but not wanting to say too much.

Baptiste threw the remnants of his coffee down and moved off towards his horse. Loughlin shook hands with Hardcastle, smiled warmly at Myra, and turned away. He helped Little Kinney up into the saddle and soon the three of them were lost from sight.

'Where's the next place we hit?' asked Myra, as they brought the wagon back on to the trail.

'Cass, I reckon. Why d'you ask?' He glanced across at her. 'You in need of somethin'?'

Myra shook her head. 'Not so's you'd notice.'

It was not far south of Cass that they ran into Wes Hart and told him how to find the Grant place, Myra suckling her child and fingering her .38 at the same time.

Nine

The morning following their first meeting with Hart, they saw him again. Wes had been up before the first light, before the first song of the birds really caught fire. He had seen to his horse and checked out his guns, dismantling the Colt and cleaning it, piece by piece, putting it back together with unhurried speed and precision.

Malcolm Grant had been waiting for him on the front porch of the house. There was ham and eggs, cornbread, good coffee. Hart watched as Grant took a couple of eggs uncooked and straight from their shells before settling down to the fried kind.

'Good for a man,' Grant had said.

Hart nodded and kept his own counsel.

During the meal, the banker gave Hart all the information he'd obtained from Marshal Fagan about the escape. How many men Majors had broken out with, some details about them – a couple of no-good niggers and three desperadoes who were behind bars for train robbery. There was only one clue to the direction the escaped prisoners might take: the train robbers were known to operate up by the Missouri border. The remnants of the Loughlin gang had been hit hard by a posse from a town called Garfield, close by Beaver Lake. Two of them had got away and as far as was known they were still on the run.

'Do you think Majors would have stayed with these men?' Grant asked.

Hart chewed on some ham and thought about it. 'I reckon. For a while at least. He'll likely reckon his chances are better than on his own.'

'So you think they'll ride north again? Up to the border country?'

'It's a chance.'

Grant sat forward. 'What sort of chance?'

Hart shrugged. 'Chance I got to take.'

The Hardcastle wagon wasn't the first thing Hart saw when he rode early into Cass, but it was one of them. He noted it, saw that neither the man nor the woman were around, and carried on down the street towards the marshal's office. He found it caught between a saloon and a saddler's, thick door reinforced with hefty planks of wood that had been nailed across it, one window that was almost too small for a man to stick his head out of without wriggling. There wasn't anything about it that looked welcoming.

Hart dismounted, tied up his horse, and hammered on the door. He was greeted by the sudden barking of what sounded to be a pretty big dog. More knocking only seemed to make the animal all the more furious, so Hart waited while a man's grumbling voice grew slowly more distinct. Eventually, it shouted through the thickness of the wood: 'Who the hell is it, this hour?'

'Name's Hart, marshal. Want to talk to you is all.'

'This ain't the marshal,' the voice grumbled. 'An' if you want to talk why don't you wait till a proper hour.'

'There's folk enough stirrin' round town,' said Hart, controlling his temper.

'Then go talk to them!'

Hart heard the man moving away from the door and the dog changed from barking to a hungry howl. Hart stepped back and lashed his foot out at the door, kicking it hard; it hardly moved against its hinges. He cursed and turned away, angry that he was going to have to waste time. Even as he turned he saw the marshal heading diagonally across the street towards him.

'What the hell you think you're doin' to that door?'

'Kickin' it.'

'I can see that!'

'Then why the hell d'you ask?'

They faced up to one another. The marshal was five or so years younger than Hart and a few inches shorter; what he lost in age and height he more than made up for in weight, a good belly sagging low against his pants belt. The leather of his gun belt strained beneath the swell of it, as if it was holding it in place. He was wearing a black leather vest with the marshal's badge pinned to it, not a six-pointed star like Fagan's United States marshal's badge, but a shield with fancy engraving to the centre.

Hart looked from badge to belly to the hand that was close to the black-wood butt of a .45.

He wasn't about to let that sagging gut fool him none. You didn't draw with your stomach.

'Want words, marshal.'

'What about?'

'Men who took off from the State Pen.'

'How in the Lord's name are they to do with me – or my door?'

'Happen they come this way.'

'Who says?'

'US Marshal Fagan for one. Malcolm Grant for another.'

The marshal cleared his throat and looked around as though he were about to spit. He didn't; he swallowed it instead. 'Why didn't you say so right off,' he said, 'instead of wastin' time?'

He stepped past Hart and on to the boardwalk, calling out to the man inside to open the door. Passing through, he glanced a shade regretfully down at the scuff mark near the bottom of the woodwork.

'Angus, what you playin' at, not lettin' folk in to see me?'

The old timer wiped a little spittle from his face and belched into the air; suddenly the place stank of old wine. 'You wasn't here,' he said.

Over towards the back corner, a tan-coloured dog with a smooth coat and a head the size of a small bull's stared at Hart and growled through clenched teeth.

Hart looked back at it, wondering if he'd be quick enough to draw his Colt and fire, before the beast could sink its teeth into his throat.

The marshal went over and patted the dog on the head and the animal lay down and looked peaceful. Still, it kept one eye on Hart, peering over the top of a paw that was folded round before its head.

'Name's Ben,' said the marshal.

'Yours?'

'No. The dog's. Mine's Tremlett. Jake Tremlett.'

'Wes Hart.'

They nodded at one another and exchanged a few pleasantries while the old man was making his exit.

'Fagan sent you up here?' asked Tremlett as the door closed.

'Not exactly.'

'What then?'

'He suggested I could do a job of work for Grant. Tracking these men down. One of 'em, anyway.'

'What's Grant's interest in escaped prisoners?'

'One of 'em raped his daughter, killed his son.'

Tremlett pursed his lips for a whistle that never came; instead, he sat down on the swivel chair behind his desk and nodded his head a few times. Hart described the other prisoners as best he could and asked the marshal if he'd seen anyone suspicious around town or passing through any time inside the last three days or so. Tremlett hadn't, but after a few minutes he reckoned it was worth telling Hart of a story he'd picked up from a rancher who worked a strip of land down past the Mulberry.

'Place name of Ozark. Heard of it?'

Hart allowed that he hadn't.

'Don't matter. Bank got held up. One of Grant's banks as it happens, though likely he don't know about it yet. Didn't get away with much, didn't manage a lot more than make fools of themselves way I heard it told. But there was four of 'em. One black, three whites. Sheriff down there, John Dillon, he got one of 'em in the back, wounded him bad so he told it. Others were lucky to get out of town. They never even got the safe open.'

Tremlett leaned back far enough in the chair to hook one of his boots up on to the edge of the desk.

'Killed a young clerk, though. Wounded woman as worked there and beat up the manager pretty bad.'

'Know which way they headed out?'

'Uh-huh,' nodded Tremlett, 'they went north.'

Hart took a couple of paces back from the desk. It didn't have to be the men he was looking for, but the time was right and the place. And if they'd been in Ozark round about . . . He went over the office to the map that was hanging from the side wall, tracing his finger north from Ozark to Cass and up from there in the direction of Garfield and the Missouri border.

'How many days ride you call it?'

'Garfield? Depends. Ridin' fast, changin' horses: two, three days.'

Hart turned away from the map. 'Not for them. They're goin' to be keeping out of sight as much as they can, they'll know the longer they stay free the more chance there is of 'em bein' spotted. This side of the border, anyway.'

Tremlett pulled his leg back from the desk top. 'Ain't but the one you're interested in, that it?'

'Lloyd Majors is all.'

'The rest?'

Hart shrugged his shoulders. 'Less'n they get in my way, I ain't got no quarrel with them.'

The marshal pushed his chair back a little, eyed Hart carefully. 'They bust out of the pen. One of 'em was due for hangin', weren't he?'

Hart stepped away. 'I ain't no lawman. Cast off my badge a time back.'

Tremlett reached towards one of the desk drawers and pulled out a bunch of fliers. The one he was looking for was close to the top. He glanced at it quickly, refreshing his memory. Then he span it round and pushed it across the desk.

The Aitchison, Topeka and Santa Fe railroad was offering a reward of five hundred dollars for the return of the money stolen from one of its trains amounting to six thousand dollars in total.

'That don't interest you?' Tremlett asked with a wry smile.

'I told you what interested me. Majors.'

'You're gettin' paid pretty good for that, huh?'

'Enough,' Hart agreed.

Tremlett stood up suddenly. 'Well,' he said, 'you can be sure there'll be those who are interested enough. An' they won't be fussy how they get what they're after. If they reckon you're beatin' 'em to it, you'd best watch your back as well as your front.'

Hart nodded. 'Thanks for the advice.'

He tipped the brim of his hat quickly with the fingers of his right hand and moved to the door. Hand on the lock, he swung back round. 'The railroad – they got their own men out?'

Tremlett smiled slowly. 'I was wonderin' when you'd ask that. Couple of 'em rode through here a day back. Pinkertons. Hired by the AT an' Santa Fe. Miserable lookin' bastards. Never cracked a smile the once. I wouldn't let either of them get too long a look at my back either.'

Hart nodded. 'Thanks again.'

Out on the street, the sun was hot, baking the packed earth. The air shimmered and the buildings more than fifty yards off seemed to shift on their foundations. The tall wagon was still where it had been when Hart had ridden into town, only this time Seymore Hardcastle was standing alongside, fixing the harness for the mules. Hart untethered the grey and walked her down the street.

'Mornin'.'

Hardcastle turned with surprise, recognized Hart immediately. He nodded a greeting and his top hat slid a couple of inches forward on his head. 'You found the Grant place okay?'

'Thanks.'

'Ridin' on now, I guess?'

'That's right.' Hart looked as far as he could through the flap of the wagon, but he could see no sign of the woman.

'She's across to the store,' said Hardcastle, reading his thoughts. 'Buyin' things for the child.'

'Uh-huh. She seems quite a woman.'

'So she is.'

Hardcastle looked past Hart to the general store across the street. At that moment, a man opened the door and Myra stepped out on to the boardwalk, lifting one arm to shield her eyes from the sun. The baby was slung across her front in a makeshift contraption which left the woman's hands free. She saw Hart and started off across the street.

'Ma'am,' said Hart, nodding in her direction.

'You didn't decide to buy some cure-all, did you?'

'No, ma'am. Just passin' the time of day.'

'Bottle wouldn't do you no harm,' said Hardcastle quickly, pleased at the possibility of a sale.

Hart shook his head. 'No offence. But I never did see how a patent medicine that's supposed to cure everythin' can be a lot of good. If it was, no one'd be goin' around sick.'

'I can't agree . . .' Hardcastle began.

'If you'd seen what it done a couple of days back, you wouldn't be sayin' that,' said Myra. 'Seymore here more or less performed an operation on two men, using that cure-all as the only help he had. They were shot-up pretty bad and . . .'

She stopped, seeing the narrowing of Hart's eyes, the shift in the level of his attention. He wasn't simply passing the time of day any more.

'These men,' said Hart, 'tell me about them.'

'Well,' Hardcastle began, 'that'd be difficult. Didn't learn their names or nothin'. They didn't give 'em and . . .'

'One of 'em, was he shot in the back? That what you worked on?'

Hardcastle nodded again and his top hat screwed round at an angle. 'Not just one of 'em, both. Both shot in the back. Strange thing, but there it was. They . . .'

'They didn't say where they was headed?'

'No, can't say . . .'

'Missouri,' Myra broke in. 'Up Missouri way, that's what he said.'

'Who said?'

'The one I was talkin' to while Seymore was tendin' to his friends.'

'Just the three of them?' asked Hart.

'Only the three.'

Hart scratched the side of his chin. If it was the men from the State Penitentiary, they'd split up pretty fast, but that wasn't too surprising. What interested him was which group Majors was in. He asked the couple to describe the men they'd seen as best they could and when they had, he didn't figure any of them for Majors. Not the way he'd heard Grant picture the man who'd killed his son.

'You interested in these men for some good reason?' asked Hardcastle.

Hart nodded. 'Good enough.'

'You a lawman?' asked Myra, beginning to regret that she'd been so free with her tongue. She remembered how much she'd enjoyed talking with the man by the fire, how much she'd enjoyed the way he'd looked at her body.

'Detective?' she asked, after Hart had shaken his head to her first question.

'That neither.'

Her face coloured with displeasure. 'You must be a bounty hunter, then.'

Hart shook his head and said he wasn't exactly that, either. Hardcastle suggested to Myra that she might be well put to mind more of her own business.

'You sure you didn't catch a name?' asked Hart, staring at the woman hard.

'I said so, didn't I?' she flushed.

'You said it, right enough. I thought maybe you'd forgot.'

'Then you thought wrong.'

Hart knew she wasn't about to say any more. And he guessed it didn't matter any too much. Wounded like they were, the three men wouldn't be making much ground. He reckoned he'd catch up to them soon enough. Then the questions would get answered so there wasn't any mistake.

He touched his hat and turned away, heading for the livery stable to make arrangements for an extra horse. Behind him, the baby woke up and started crying and Myra struggled with her bad temper, taking the child into the wagon out of the heat. Hardcastle was looking at Hart, thinking that he wouldn't care to be in any of those fellers' boots when Hart caught up with them.

Ten

Hardcastle couldn't have known that Hart wasn't going to be the one who caught up to Loughlin and the others first. No one could. The chances of the two Pinkertons finding them weren't a whole lot better than Hart's. Sure, they had the advantage of time and distance, but they didn't have such a close idea of the way Loughlin was travelling. Some folk think that once you call a man a detective, instead of a sheriff or marshal, or some other kind of lawman, that makes him something special. Singles him out as different, someone clever with his head, expert at tracking a person down and brighter than most at figuring out the whys and the wherefores of things.

It isn't necessarily true.

About the only time Hart had run into a detective was when he was messing with the Lee Sternberg gang. There'd been a man name of Fowler – Hart had got to like him well enough. He'd even turned up with a trump card or two in the end, but he wouldn't have said this Fowler had any special brainpower working for him. Most the only thing he had working for him was bourbon, and he drank so much of that in the course of a day that it was a wonder he could stand at all.

As a matter of fact, a lot of the time he couldn't. Just about the first occasion Hart even met him, Fowler fell flat on his face.

Even so, he was a decent enough feller, which was more than anyone had ever said about Charlie Deuce and Norton Carey. When Tremlett said neither of them cracked a smile, it had been no less than the truth. He'd been pretty close when he'd made his warning about not showing either of them too much back as well.

Charlie Deuce, he'd been a Pinkerton since the War Between the States, stuck with the agency even when they were having a bad time for losing more of the federal government's secrets than they found from the Confederacy. The life suited him and he was tolerably good at it. He was a slim, thin-faced man with short-cropped grey hair and eyes that were cold as steel and cut right through a man like a well-honed knife. Deuce, he carried a little Remington on a hinged frame inside his sleeve. Tapped the frame on a table or some such and the gun snapped out plumb into the palm of the hand. Apart from that, all he had was a pair of rifles, sat either side of his saddle. One – the one he favoured – was a Sharps .55, the other a Henry carbine. Deuce liked the Sharps better on account of it was accurate over one hell of a distance. With that weapon, and with the wind in the right direction, he could kill a man without even having so much as seen his face. Now, to Charlie Deuce, that was the way detecting should be.

Norton Carey was six or seven years younger, twenty or so pounds heavier. He'd been a Pinkerton for less than three years and he'd been teamed with Deuce for the last two of those. Carey came from the north-east and he'd started his working life as a

'Light out.'

Tap let the smoke drift upwards from his mouth and nostrils. He held the cigarette cupped inside the curve of his right hand.

'That weren't . . .'

'Yes, it was. We been together too long for you to start lyin' to me now.'

Tap drew deep on the cigarette and tried not to feel whatever it was that was twisting inside his gut.

'You done what you could,' said Baptiste, 'but it wasn't the right thing.'

There was anger in Tap's face when he turned, anger in his voice and all of it directed against himself. 'You know I ain't scarcely done a thing right since we took that train. Tried to take the damned train. Look at what happened since we broke out – what happened to you, to Kinney in there. That's what I done!'

Baptiste shook his head, set his broad hand against the top of Tap's shoulder. 'You never done that. Neither of those things. It weren't your fault. None of it.' He moved his hand away. 'Don't blame yourself.'

Tap nodded, but what the big man said didn't do anything to make him feel any more at peace with himself.

'We'll make out,' said Baptiste after a few moments during which the only sound was of Little Kinney groaning.

'Yeah!' laughed Tap. 'Two cripples proppin' one another up. You'll fare pretty good, okay.'

'Time you stopped mindin' other folks business for 'em. You get on one of them horses come sun-up and ride the hell out of here. There's a lot of dollars up by the border and it's yours to get.'

'Yours and Kinney's too.'

'Fine. You get to it before that mad dog Majors and keep it for us till we get fixed up and get there.'

The two men stared at one another through the half-light; Kinney moaned again inside the shack.

'I know that ain't all as is crossin' your mind,' Baptiste went on.

Tap turned away, dragged on the cigarette.

'It's her, ain't it?'

'Her?'

'That teacher. That Sara-Lee. You're frightened he's goin' to get to the money through her.'

'He won't!' Tap's voice was firm, hard: not hard enough to convince Baptiste, certainly not enough to convince himself.

'You're a fool!' snorted Baptiste. 'Ride out!'

But Tap turned on him again, throwing the cigarette butt down to the ground. 'That man in there,' he pointed at the shack, his face tight with anger, 'he had a chance to ride off back in Ozark. I ain't forgettin' what he did for me.'

'Yeah,' said Baptiste. 'Yeah, sure. He saved your life just to have you throw it away again.'

The big man shuffled slowly back inside, leaving Tap Loughlin to his own thoughts, the sliver of moon, the coming cold of the night.

Charlie Deuce and Norton Carey picked up the tracks of three horses moving slow just before dusk settled in too far for them to make out anything more than their own hoofbeats.

'What d'you reckon?' asked Carey, leaning back in the saddle and stretching his back, reaching one hand round to rub it at the centre. It had been a long day, they'd been on the move since first light, cross-checking the tracks each side of the northern trail.

Charlie Deuce shifted his weight, pushed his fingers up through his close-cut hair. 'One carrying more weight than the others?'

'Looks like.'

'Same as we saw yesterday then lost?'

'Uh-huh.'

Deuce reached round to one of his saddle bags and unbuckled a strap; he fingered out a small silver flask and snapped out the cork. Wiping the neck with his sleeve, he set the flask to his mouth and swallowed twice. He stoppered the flask and slid it back from sight without ever thinking to offer a drink to his partner.

'We're not goin' to see much in this light.'

'That's true enough.'

'Hardly a thing.'

'No.'

Charlie Deuce sighed elaborately and shifted across the saddle again. He lifted his silver case watch from a vest pocket and snapped the front open.

'Let's give it another hour.'

He shut the watch and dropped it back down into his pocket. It was seven minutes short of the hour when they saw the smoke.

Charlie Deuce sat huddled under the plain blanket he kept wrapped inside an oilskin slicker at the back of his saddle. He'd long since taken off his boots and pulled on two more pairs of long wool socks; he had put on a pair of thick gloves and sat on his saddle bags. Watching. The brandy in his flask had run out half-way through the night. It had been a long time since the couple of men who'd been standing out by the horses had had their conversation and then gone back inside.

Alongside, Norton Carey had let his head droop a number of times, fading into sleep and coming out of it again with a start and a quickly muffled sound from his lips. Carey had been all of going down right off – soon as they'd had time to get to sleep at least – and blasting into them. Charlie Deuce had been against it. For one thing they weren't certain who exactly was in there; for another, if they made their move at night then it would be easier for the men to slip away.

No, they would wait until just before dawn. That would be the best time. Carey might have argued some more but he didn't see the sense to it. No amount of words were ever going to change Deuce's mind once it was set – that was one of the things Carey admired about him most.

So Carey gripped his arms tight across his chest and did his best not to let it appear that he was shivering. Charlie Deuce wasn't the kind of man you showed any sign of weakness to: if you did then sooner or later he'd turn it against you. That was something else Carey admired about the man.

Down inside the shack everything was quiet; the fire had embered out and even Little Kinney had managed to get some sleep.

It was shattered by the thump of something landing on the floor of the shack, something hurled through the single window, ripping through the tattered piece of sacking that had been nailed across it.

Little Kinney was the closest to consciousness, the first to react. He tried to sit up from his blanket, yelled as he realized that with his back in the state it was, there was no way he was going to be able to do that. He rolled on to his side instead and shouted all the louder.

Tap and Baptiste were awake seconds later, alerted by Kinney's shouted warnings and by the smell of burning.

The blazing rags that had been hurled through the window had been soaked in paraffin and fixed to a length of branch. Thick black smoke spluttered all over the interior. The three men moved as best they could, Tap jumping to his feet and trying to seize the brand and throw it back out, but the flames had caught too well now and he wasn't able to get that close. He tried kicking at it, shifting it towards the door. All three men were yelling warnings, orders, questions. Baptiste finally threw his blanket over the blaze and stomped down on it with his bare feet.

The first volley of shots burst through the front of the shack: only the door was stout enough to deflect the bullets, the rest tore through the thin warped timber and into the sod wall at the side, the bare surface of the hill behind.

'Jesus!'

'Who the hell?'

Tap and Baptiste grabbed their guns and moved towards the front wall, only too aware that another round of shooting could rip into them.

'The horses!' shouted Kinney, struggling into his boots best as he could. 'Get the horses!'

Tap turned away from the window. 'The horses are gone.'

'Don't be a fool! How can they?'

Tap shook his head, a grim smile showing around his mouth. 'They're gone.'

'Bastards!' Baptiste eased the door back a few inches and immediately two shots rang out. He ducked back below the splintering wood and cursed some more.

'Come out now and keep your hands high!'

'Throw out your guns!'

The blanket had failed to smother the fire completely; flames were starting to lick out from beneath the edges, yellow and orange and curling. Dark smoke once again drifted around the inside of the shack.

Little Kinney snapped a last shell into the chamber of his pistol, coughed hard, shuffled towards the corner of the front wall. When he leaned his head against it and coughed again, bright blood flecked across the soiled board.

'You got another ten seconds.'

Baptiste and Tap exchanged quick glances.

'I'll cover you,' said Baptiste. 'We'll hold 'em off while you make it far as you can.'

'Without a horse?' scoffed Loughlin.

'Okay. Stay here an' get shot to pieces.'

Tap eased his gun over the sill of the window. 'Damn it! We'll stay together.'

'You're a fool!'

Their ten seconds were up and there weren't going to be any second chances, no more warnings. Rifle shots peppered the shack, tearing through the decaying timbers. Baptiste and Tap gave as good an answering fire as they could, picking out the positions, right and left, the firing was coming from. Whoever it was was keeping well under cover, almost out of sixgun range, not taking any chances.

'Bastards!' roared Baptiste again and emptied his gun through a slit in the wall, leaning back and reaching for fresh cartridges.

Tap was already on his knees, reloading, one side of his face welling with blood where a sliver of wood had pierced his cheek. His left arm had taken a deep graze and was stinging sharply, more blood running free down to the elbow and from there to the floor.

Little Kinney still hadn't moved from the corner; his head was still pressed against the wood and his mouth was open, like a fish thrown up on the shore. His eyes were open too, but they weren't seeing anything any longer. As many as four bullets had driven into him, three of them lodging fast. His shirt, his vest, his pants were wet with blood, sticky with it, stinking with it. He slumped in a rising puddle of it. It didn't seem that there would be any left long in his whole body, he was leaking blood so fast.

'Jesus!' Tap started across the floor towards Kinney but halfway there he stopped himself, knowing the uselessness of it.

'If you're still alive in there, throw out your guns and come on out after 'em!'

Baptiste shook his head, coughed. The blanket was just smouldering now, the flames dying; the room swam with smoke.

'Who d'you reckon it is?' he asked.

Tap shook his head; he looked exhausted, broken.

'Like to know,' said Baptiste, pushing himself slowly up the wall to his feet. 'Like to know who it is I'm gettin' killed by.'

Tap saw that he'd taken at least another bullet; some of the blood seeping through his clothing was new, differently placed.

'Some damn posse,' said Tap, shaking his head.

'How in hell's name they know who we are?'

'Maybe they don't.'

Baptiste shook his head low; for almost the first time since he had known him, Tap thought he looked about to give in.

'You got your last chance!' boomed the voice from the hill.

Tap Loughlin stood upright, pistol in his right hand. His throat was constricted and dry and he still didn't know what the hell he was going to do and why, except that sure as anything he wasn't about to throw out that gun and go walking after it. He sure wasn't about to do that.

'All right.' Baptiste had moved to the corner of the room and retrieved Little Kinney's pistol. He checked the chamber and pushed it down into his belt. His own pistol was in his left hand; the shotgun now in his right. He looked at Tap and nodded in the direction of the back of the shack.

'No!' Tap said, even before the big man's thoughts had been articulated.

'Them boards. They're rotten. You can easy bust through. The horses can't be far. You take one and get the hell out.'

'I . . .'

'Go see Sara-Lee.'

Air sucked hard from Tap's body. Baptiste grinned through his heavy beard and moved to the door. The last thing Tap saw of him was that big leg swinging back and kicking the door open, then striding out into the early light. Tap ducked towards the rear of the shack.

Outside, Baptiste stood for a moment drawing in the bright cold of the air. He glimpsed a second's reflection of metal on the hillside to the left, another slight movement amongst a group of trees right of centre. He knew the way things were whoever was there was too far out of range.

What he needed was a little more distance.

Holding that fresh air down in his lungs, Baptiste started to walk forward. Shotgun and pistol were held low down by his legs and he made no attempt to lift them higher. Six paces, seven, nine, improbably eleven. He seemed to be stepping out into some kind of dream, Tap, Little Kinney, everything so quickly fading back of him. Even the pain that nagged at his back, the lesser, nagging pains in his leg seemed to have diminished almost to nothing. Ahead of him, through the clump of trees, the hazy orange of the sun was coming up like one of the big sternwheelers back down by New Orleans.

The shots came from both directions more or less at once and rocked him this way and that and the big man's knees shook and gave a couple of inches but no more.

Baptiste swung up the pistol now, aiming at the shape barely glimpsed by the trunk of a tree and then swinging it round towards the hill.

He gritted his teeth and took another step, another. A slug ripped through his body inches above the hip and he sucked in his lower lip and bit down into it hard enough to raise blood.

As if there weren't blood enough!

He saw one of the rifles clear and tried to hold his right arm steady enough to draw a bead but another bullet plucked at his chest and threw him off balance. One more wavering pace and he doubled over, resting his weight on the shortened barrels of the unfired shotgun.

A slug spurted dirt up into his face where it ploughed into the earth a couple of inches in front of him.

Baptiste was breathing heavily now, his whole body shaking with the lumbering effort of it; he was like a wounded bison at the moment before the beast keeled over on to the ground.

The two detectives held their fire and waited for that moment.

Baptiste trembled, shivered the bent length of his body, but he didn't keel over. Instead he pulled himself straight and started off again towards the trees. He was firing the sixgun as he walked, knowing that he might only get one of the men, but if he could do that . . .

He thought he was being hit as he went forward, but he couldn't any longer be sure. He could still see the sun behind the trees but it looked mistier than ever and the trunks and branches seemed to be swimming in a kind of orange fire. Bathing in it. He choked on a mouthful of phlegm and blood and hawked it to his feet. Something kicked into his belly and he staggered back, right arm waving wildly. The already empty gun fell from his fingers and he tried to reach the other at his belt.

A slug slammed into his shoulder-blade from behind and he was driven to his knees with a thud that jolted pain screaming through his entire body.

Baptiste brought up his head and then the shotgun, finger across the trigger, right hand coming round to steady the twin barrels.

A rifle bullet smacked into the side of his face and sharded his cheekbone away, pulped mouth and ear against what remained of the back of his skull.

Baptiste emptied both barrels into the orange haze of the sun, blasting it out of the sky. He fell like dead weight into the darkness he had created.

Eleven

Charlie Deuce touched the door with the stock of his rifle and it fell away from the remaining hinge and skidded up dirt and dust. Deuce waited for it to settle and stepped inside. The stink of burning clung to the ceiling and the stench of blood was hued to the walls.

The Pinkerton man's eyes took in the body slumped into the corner, the boards ripped away. He narrowed his already narrow eyes and pressed his lips together until all the blood was forced from them. He cursed several times inside his head and walked across to Little Kinney's body.

Using the long barrel of the Sharps he lifted the man's head high enough to get a look at the face. A pair of dead eyes, one blue, one green, stared back up at him.

Deuce looked into them for a few moments before letting the head fall. He went to the open doorway.

Carey was kneeling beside Baptiste's inert body, trying to count the number of bullet holes front and back.

'We missed one of 'em,' said Deuce, each word flat and lifeless as Baptiste's body. Somehow more so.

Carey nodded, registering what his partner said without reacting. 'You know,' he said a moment later, 'there must be fifteen, sixteen slugs in this big ox's body.'

'Got away,' said Deuce. 'Bust through the back while this was going on and got clear away.'

Carey stood up, brushing the dirt from his pants. 'Could be if we look round, we'll find he's got no further than the nearest ditch.'

'We'll look all right, but we won't find him.'

Carey looked at him questioningly.

'Those horses wouldn't have run far. We should've hobbled them while there was time.'

Carey shrugged. 'Didn't figure it was going to be an issue.'

'No. Didn't figure that bull there for doing what he did.'

The two detectives stared at Baptiste for a moment, his inert body still leaking blood into the soil.

'Why d'you think he done that?' asked Carey.

'Why?' Deuce came a few paces closer, shading his eyes from the sun. 'Why? How the hell should I know why? He went berserk. Ran amok. Who knows why men like that know what they do.'

Carey shook his head, rubbed the side of his jaw. 'Almost as if . . .' he began and then stopped.

'As if what?'

'As if he done it on purpose. Came out and drew our fire so's whoever was still alive in there could get away.'

Charlie Deuce let the idea run through his mind for a little, but not for long. He couldn't see the sense in it. Nor, to tell the truth, could Norton Carey. The two detectives soon shunted the thought from their minds for good.

'We get Loughlin?' asked Carey, coming down towards the shack.

'I don't think so. It certainly isn't the one out front, doubt if it's him inside. Descriptions don't fit with what we got.'

Carey rubbed his chin, turned in the doorway. 'You think Loughlin was the other one?'

Deuce looked past him towards the spot where the boards had been torn away. 'Who knows? We can check the tracks. Make sure it was only one got away and one of them horses weren't carrying double. Do what we got to do here and take off after him.'

Carey looked at Deuce with his head set to one side. 'We ain't buryin' these two, are we? No point in haulin' 'em all over the country, neither.'

'We'll make sure there ain't no money stashed around. They took a bank down south, remember, even if they didn't get free with much. Then we'll drag the guts in here and give this place the torch. Even that's more'n what they deserve.'

The timber was little more than a blackened shell when Hart came to the ridge of land behind the trees. He was astride the grey, a long-legged pinto that he'd hired out from the livery on a rope behind. Riding the horses in turn, he'd made good time. Sleeping just a few hours and moving off again before dawn had helped too. He'd seen the smoke from the burning building for a good couple of miles now, changing trails towards it with an ever-increasing feeling in his gut that he was heading towards something important.

The two men were sitting away from the fire, positioned clear of the smoke that was being tugged by the wind. They'd built a small blaze of their own and looked to have been breakfasting well. Hart could catch the occasional tang of saltback bacon and the smell of good coffee.

Hart stared down at the shack and wondered what had been burned inside it; he thought about the distant gunfire he'd heard earlier. The way he had it figured, the two men below must reckon they'd earned their good meal.

He slipped the leather thong free from the hammer of his Colt .45, shrugged back the Indian blanket from his left shoulder so that it trailed behind and he was free to move his hand to the holstered sawn-off.

Clicking his tongue at the grey, he set off down the slope.

He hadn't made more than a few yards before both men had sat up, jumped up, made a move towards their weapons. Hart lifted both hands clear for a moment to show he had no intentions of going for his own guns, then returned them to reins and saddle pommel.

'That's close enough, stranger.'

Hart looked at Charlie Deuce as the detective spoke and nodded in reply, but didn't stop.

'I said . . .'

'I heard what you said,' snapped Hart. 'I just wonder what you got to be so damned jumpy about.'

Hart was no more than ten yards off now and he brought Clay to a halt. The pinto shuffled alongside, turned its head towards that of the grey, sniffed the air, then backed off a few strides and pawed the earth, shaking its mane.

'Sometimes,' said Carey, stroking his pistol butt almost negligently, 'it don't pay to let folk get too close till you know what they've a mind to.'

Hart nodded, grinned. 'I heard that.' The grin disappeared as swiftly as it had come.

'What's your business?' asked Deuce, angling his right arm

round so as to be able to use the hideaway deringer if necessary.

Hart followed the move and guessed the reason behind it. Another smile flickered across his face. 'Maybe,' he said evenly, 'it's the same as yours.'

Charlie Deuce lifted his enamel mug from by his polished boots and held it in both hands; he set it to his mouth and spoke over the rim. 'You saying you're a lawman?'

Hart wasn't saying anything.

'Show us your badge,' said Carey.

'You got a spare cup of coffee?' asked Hart. 'Sure is a cold mornin' after the heat we had last couple of days.'

Carey spat, neatly and precisely, into the centre of the fire. 'Got a lot of gall.'

'Else he's a mite short on sense,' suggested Deuce, talking about Hart as though he weren't there.

'How 'bout that coffee?' Hart repeated.

Carey shrugged, threw what remained in his mug over his shoulder and shook it clear. He tossed the mug up towards Hart with his left hand and set his right firm on the butt of his pistol. Smiling, Hart caught the mug with his left hand and mirrored the gesture with his right.

When the move was stalemated, Hart swung down from the saddle, keeping his gunhand clear to move.

Charlie Deuce, unsmiling, poured black coffee from the pot.

'We got sugar,' said Carey.

'Uh-uh. Thanks.'

Hart stood and drank; the coffee was nearly as good as it had smelt. He was sorry that he'd arrived too late for the bacon. His eyes drifted towards the burned-out shack. Sorry he'd arrived too late for other things.

'You were saying something about how we might have, er, mutual interests,' said Deuce, looking at Hart keenly.

'Uh-huh. Could be.' He drank some more coffee and let the pair of them wait a little longer.

Hart didn't like the look of either man and he certainly didn't trust them. What the lawman had said back in Cass about not turning his back made a whole lot of sense now that he met up with these two face to face. The older one didn't appear to be carrying a gun, which meant that he surely was and that it was stashed away somewhere, ready to take someone unsuspecting by surprise. From one of his movements earlier, Hart figured the man to have one of them little deringers up his sleeve – he wouldn't have been surprised if there weren't another in a shoulder rig. The second man had a Smith & Wesson Schofield holstered high on his right hip and the way he was hugging it suggested there wasn't much else he'd rather do than put it to some use right there. From the bulge under his black coat, Hart didn't have to guess at the presence of a shoulder holster – he could see it and be certain.

He still wanted to know what else was burning inside that old shack.

'Working for the railroad, huh?' he asked, keeping his voice on the lazy side.

The two men glanced at one another and after a moment, the grey-haired one said: 'That's a possibility.'

Hart tossed the remnants of the coffee into the fire and the flames hissed and spat little yellow flames. 'Possibility, shit! You're ridin' for the Aitchison and Topeka. You ain't likely regular railroad detectives, you probably draw your pay from the Pinkerton Agency, that'd be the way the railroad would do it. You're chasin' down the bunch that broke out of the State Pen on account of the fact they made a pass at one of the AT and Santa Fe's trains and there's still around six thousand dollars runnin' loose.' Hart paused and looked from one man to the other. 'Now you tell me to hold my tongue if I'm talkin' out of turn.'

Charlie Deuce got up. He did it slow enough and neat enough and the expression on his face never changed. Hart reckoned it was some kind of signal between them and he didn't want to get caught in the middle of some snappy cross-fire. He took a couple of paces back and let his body drop into the beginnings of a crouch. His right arm curved out from his side, the fingers arched and perched above the pearl handle of the Colt Peacemaker; his eyes were little more than slits in his face.

'I ain't interested in nothin' more than talkin',' he said. 'But if you want to insist . . .'

Deuce and Carey exchanged another glance, quicker, sharper than before. Charlie Deuce stared at Hart hard enough to cut an ordinary man, make him turn away. Hart kept on looking. After a while, Deuce sat back down.

'What's your interest?' he said.

Hart nodded beyond them at the charred shell. 'Who was in there when it took fire?'

'Couple from the Pen,' Carey answered.

'Ran with the train gang,' said Deuce.
'Loughlin's gang,' Carey went on.
'We tried to take 'em in.'
'Peaceable.'
'Gave 'em every chance to come out.'
'Didn't take it.'
'Shame.'
'Every chance.' Carey shook his head as if he were, indeed, disappointed and upset.
'That all there was?' Hart asked. 'Two?'
'Ye . . .' Deuce began, but Carey had already started: 'One other.'
Deuce gave his partner one of those looks and Carey turned his head aside and fidgeted with his belt buckle.
'That one,' said Hart, 'that would be Loughlin?'
Carey wasn't about to say anything. Deuce took a clay pipe from his side pocket and reached for a sack of tobacco. He pushed some stuff into the bowl and began to tamp it down, taking his time.
'Could have been Loughlin,' he said eventually. 'No way of knowing for certain.'
He struck a match and held it above the pipe, flame hovering. 'You still didn't say what your interest was in all this.'
'Okay. When Loughlin's bunch broke out they took a couple of blacks with 'em and a feller named Majors. Lloyd Majors. He's the one I'm interested in.'
'How come?'
Hart told them, briefly, about Grant, mentioning Marshal Fagan along the way; he didn't figure that would hurt any.
Deuce drew on his pipe. 'The train money – that don't hold no interest for you at all?'
Hart laughed: it wasn't a sound either of the detectives were used to overmuch. They looked at Hart as though he'd just farted in church. 'I come across six thousand dollars, I ain't goin' to leave it lay.'
'What are you going to do?' asked Carey, turning back into the conversation.
'Why, turn it into you fellers and claim the reward. What else would a law-abidin' citizen do with six thousand dollars of the railroad's money?'
Hart laughed again and his eyes shone as they reflected the blue of the sky; small lines etched themselves away from the corners of

his eyes and mouth. He was still laughing when he swung back into the saddle and touched the brim of his hat. 'Good-day, gents. Obliged for the coffee. If I catch up with this Loughlin before you, I'll be sure and tell him you're lookin' for him.' He turned the grey around, pulling on the pinto's rope. 'And if I find that money . . .'

Hart's voice died on the wind. Charlie Deuce stood up fast and stared after him; he looked down at Carey and said: 'Get this gear stashed away. Gone time we were on the move. We just might teach that cocksure bastard a lesson!'

Twelve

Tap Loughlin followed the course of the White River up towards Beaver Lake; once the lake was in sight, he'd ride along the western shore and drive north towards Garfield. Except that Garfield wasn't a place he intended to visit. That was where the remnants of his gang had come to grief and Tap didn't fancy adding to that total. He would skirt round it and get himself across into Missouri as fast as he could. Once there he had a pretty good idea where Jeff and Bluey would have hid out, where they would have stashed the money. And that was awful close to Springfield. He saw the foam bubbling where the river water hit the rocks and saw Sara-Lee's smile in the middle of it, heard her laugh. Oh, God! What did it matter if she sat up in bed reading some damn play by Shakespeare till the candle guttered and died?

It didn't matter a two-cent damn.

Tap had been moving off the trail at intervals, checking the land at his rear. Occasionally he'd seen sign of what might be pursuit. One rider coming on alone – what looked like a pair of men riding together. He didn't have to work hard to guess who they might be. No, he didn't have to guess at all. Whoever had trapped Baptiste, Little Kinney and himself inside that shack wasn't about to give up. He could still hear the shooting echoing through his memory, the firing that had been going on when he'd sneaked out the back and made a run for it. All those bullets hailing into Baptiste – more than most anything else he was relieved he hadn't had to see that. See the big man's body riddled the way it must have been.

Tap pushed his tongue up against his teeth, fidgeting with a piece of dried beef that had got trapped. Baptiste had died for him, given his life so's he could get free. All right, he owed him to stay as far from the law as he could. And that pair of riders, they were the law certain. Some kind of law, private as like as not. Railroad detectives, likely.

Tap freed the beef and spat it to the ground.

Let them try and catch him. Let them ride their animals till they dropped. They wouldn't get him in a stinking fire-trap again; wouldn't catch him at all.

When he checked back down the trail next they were still there, two puffs of dust like tiny clouds rising off the land. Losing ground. Tap smiled: he hadn't seen sight of the other man's dust for seven or eight hours. Either he'd given up or he hadn't been interested in him anyway. Whatever the case, Tap felt pretty bucked.

He was still feeling good when he read the board stuck up alongside the trail that read COOPERS STAND ONE MILE UP AHEAD. As soon as he saw it his throat felt more parched and the trail dust seemed to clog the back of his throat. He had time for a couple of beers and maybe a plate of stew, something to keep him going until he reached the lake. He might even be able to do a deal with the horse, throw in what cash he had left and get a fresh mount. That would give him even more of an edge than he had already.

Cooper's Stand had been on the west bank of the river some fifteen years and in that time it had changed owners four times. Twice that had been occasioned by the untimely death of the proprietor, once it had been lost in a game of five-card stud and in the last instance the cause had been a heart-attack, brought about by lifting a heavy barrel of beer off the back of a flat-bed wagon.

No one remembered who Cooper was and where he'd come from. All that remained of him was his name, which is more than most men get to claim in the way of immortality.

On the day that Tap rode up and hitched his horse to the rail that ran at a diagonal to the front door, there was quite a crowd inside. Aside from Seth Franklin, who was the present owner, there were a couple of cowhands from a spread over the river to the east, a whisky drummer who'd lost his way travelling to Fort Smith and had been holed up for three days now, patiently working his way through his samples; there were a man and woman who were travelling by buckboard from Memphis to Joplin to collect on the man's inheritance; a couple of travellers who'd ridden up independently and were now standing up to the bar and talking together over a couple of shots of whisky.

Quite a crowd.

Tap Loughlin checked the pistol tucked into his belt and, instinctively, glanced back the way he'd come. The trail was in sight for a good way and it was clear. He shrugged his shoulders, allowed himself a smug grin, and pushed open the door.

Inside, he gave the customers the once over and stepped up to the bar.

Seth Franklin excused himself from the conversation about the relative merits of Winchesters and Henrys and asked Tap what was his pleasure.

Tap said it would be a beer followed by another beer.

He laughed and Franklin tugged at one of his drooping ear lobes and laughed along with him. It paid to keep the customers satisfied.

Tap swallowed half the contents of the glass and turned so that his back was leaning against the edge of the bar. The whisky drummer raised a glass a little shakily in his direction and Tap returned the salute. Somewhere, he could smell food cooking. A pot of stew simmering on the stove; he imagined thick chunks of potato, pieces of beef, the juice thick and bubbling. He drank another mouthful of beer and turned to ask the bartender for some food.

With a start, he realized that one of the men who'd been talking down the bar had moved in close. Tall, broad-shouldered, high cheekbones that stretched the tanned skin tight across his cheeks, eyes a faded blue that held a man and didn't let him go.

Tap's breath caught deep in his throat.

'Let's talk,' Hart said, his voice low and friendly.

Tap started for his gun and a hand shot forward and fingers seized his wrist hard, trapping it still against his chest.

'Not here,' said Hart. 'Not with so many folk around.'

The pressure on Tap's wrist increased rather than diminished. The solitary rider back down the trail, Tap was thinking, the one I'd shaken off, the one I hadn't picked up for hours. Well, that was why. He got round in front.

'Just talk,' said Hart. 'Nothin' more.'

Tap looked at the faded blue eyes disbelievingly.

'I ain't interested in you. Nor the railroad money.' Hart released his grip. 'Majors is the one I'm after.'

Tap blinked and drew a deep breath. Hart took the glass of beer from the counter and set it back in Tap's right hand.

'Okay,' said Tap, nodding. 'Okay.'

Hart smiled quickly, picked up his own drink and followed Tap to a table close to the door. The drummer waved a bottle at them as they passed and Hart gave him a look that should have scared him sober.

Tap sat down hesitantly, his tongue edging out nervously on to his lips. He searched Hart's face for some sign of weakness, of sympathy: there was none. Hart leaned one elbow on the table, pushed back his hat brim with the opposite hand.

'Came past your friends a while back,' Hart said evenly.

'Friends?'

'What was left of 'em.' The eyes narrowed. 'Ashes to ashes.'

'Who are you?' Tap jerked his head forward as he spoke.

'You was lucky not to be in there with 'em, way I heard it.'

'Who . . . ?'

'Wes Hart. I'm lookin' for a man named Majors.'

Tap Loughlin blinked fast and his head settled back. 'Majors?'

'You heard me.'

'Sure, I . . .'

'You bust out of jail with him. Thought you might know where he'd be.'

Tap turned sideways in the chair. He was full of indignation over what Majors had done to him; seething at the prospect of what he might do to Sara-Lee if he found her. He was also wondering what his chances were of sneaking the pistol out of his belt.

'I don't know where the bastard is!' he half-shouted. Two or three heads swung round his way.

'Rode off an' left you, huh?'

'Somethin' like that. I don't care what the bastard does!'

'Or where he's goin'?'

Tap pressed the palms of both hands hard against the edge of the table. 'What's that to me?' He never began to sound convincing.

Hart grinned and set his chair back on its hind legs. He was wondering how much time he had on the Pinkerton men, how long he could afford to let Loughlin take his own time.

'Share a cell with a man,' Hart said, conversationally, 'things get said that'd normally stay quiet. Stuff about that money, for instance.'

'Money?'

'Railroad money.'

'I'd . . .'

Hart's hand moved faster than Tap could follow. The fingers caught at the front of Loughlin's shirt and gripped it fast, hauling him across the table until his face was so close that Hart could feel and smell his breath, smell the taint of fear high upon it. Behind the bar Seth Franklin thought about opening the drawer where he kept his pistol stashed. Two cowhands held their breath and stared expectantly.

'What d'you think them two who put paid to your friends are out for? A little exercise? Shooting practice? You're a small-time thief, Loughlin, and the only time you tried for something bigger it bit back harder'n you could handle. But there's a lot of money hid away somewhere and you can bet those two back there somewhere ain't about to let you ride safely home an' find it. An' Majors ain't wanderin' round Arkansas catchin' flies, neither. He's chasin' them dollars down same as everyone else.' Hart relaxed his grip a little. 'Everyone 'cept me.'

The last words were spoken soft, so quiet that Tap hardly heard them. When they had registered, he looked at Hart questioningly, disbelievingly.

'What do you want, then?' he finally asked, catching his breath and shifting awkwardly back in his chair.

'Majors.'

'Majors! That bastard! What the hell for?'

'For what he did. You know 'bout that, don't you?'

Tap hawked phlegm from the back of his throat, aimed at one of the two cuspidors and nearly hit it right. He knew what Majors had done. 'You ain't a lawman. You ain't wearin' no badge.'

Hart shook his head. The cowboys had lost interest by now and were dealing from a dog-eared deck of cards. The whisky drummer had started to sing an Irish ballad. Seth Franklin hadn't got any further with his pistol than thinking about it – the way the man with the scarf and the flat-crowned hat was handling himself he could clear his pearl-handled Colt from leather so quick nothing Franklin could do was going to make any difference.

'Detective?' asked Tap.

Hart shook his head again. 'I'm workin' for the man whose kids Majors attacked. He doesn't figure it right someone like him should be runnin' free.'

Tap scratched his thigh along the top. 'Neither do I,' he said.

'Maybe you should have thought of that when you helped him get out.'

Tap nodded ruefully. 'I damn well should.'

Franklin came over and set a plate of stew in front of Loughlin, giving Hart a sideways glance as he did so. Tap pushed his fork around in the stew for a while, but his appetite had left him some minutes back.

'I'm playin' this straight,' said Hart. 'If I weren't I could take you in and hand you over to the Pinks and get a share of the reward. I could sit you on that horse out there and ride you north till you showed me where the money is – I don't want that money. I don't want you.' He pointed a finger, rock steady, into Tap's face. 'You help me find Majors, I'll let you take your chances. That's all I'm sayin'.'

Tap wrinkled up one side of his face. 'If I don't?'

Hart didn't need to answer; he simply carried on staring at Loughlin, that was enough.

'All right. We had a place, ten miles north-east of Pierce City. It's high off the Springfield road. High as anything is round there. Place called Shadow Point. Nothing more than a wooded bluff, small stream running down from it towards the James. Easy enough to spot once you know what you're lookin' for. Only one narrow trail in, though, and a couple of men could hold off a good-sized posse for a long time. I reckon that's where they'll have made a run to – Jeff and Bluey – still holed up there, I shouldn't wonder.'

'Anyone riding with Majors likely to know that?'

Tap nodded grudgingly. 'Yeah. Feller name of Levy. Scott Levy.'

'Uh-huh. Who else Majors got with him?'

'Couple of niggers is all.'

Hart drummed his fingers on the table and stood up. 'Them Pinkertons,' he said, 'you run your own chance with them. I'd say you take your time, you'll get wherever you're goin' right enough. There are ways of avoidin' bein' caught. And they'll be keepin' more'n half an eye on that money anyhow.'

Tap nodded. 'Thanks.'

'Okay.' Hart turned away and glanced quickly back over his shoulder. If Loughlin had been considering making a play for his gun, he would have done it then. But his right hand was still toying with a fork, his left was idle on his knee.

'Be seein' you, maybe,' Hart said, and stepped through the door.

He was pulling himself up into the saddle when Loughlin appeared. Hart's gun was in his hand so quick it made Tap gasp and stagger a couple of paces back.

'Take it easy!' he called.

'You be careful how you come through doors,' warned Hart.

Tap came closer to the rail. 'One thing.'

'Yeah?'

'This Majors – you reckon you'll get him? I mean, you can deal with him okay?'

Hart shrugged. 'I took the job. That's enough for me.'

'Fine, only . . .'

'Yeah?'

Loughlin didn't like saying it and when he did it tumbled out all of a piece, but Hart got the gist of it anyhow. 'This girl, woman, she's a teacher. Up in Springfield. Name's Danziger. Sara-Lee Danziger. Her an' me . . . anyhow, Majors, he knows about her. What you was sayin' 'bout folk who share cells sayin' more'n they should. I reckon he might think she knows about the money or . . . or even if he don't there's somethin' makes me . . . he'll seek her out. I'm all but sure of that. Seek her out an' . . .'

Loughlin's eyes flickered across Hart's face and quickly away, as though afraid that Hart would somehow be able to see pictured there what was happening in Loughlin's mind.

Hart could smell fear rising off the man again, only this time it was for somebody else as well as himself.

'You catch up with Majors and he'll never get to Springfield.'

Hart nodded. 'Maybe. I ain't making promises.'

'You could . . .'

'I can do what I can do. Nothin' more.' Hart pulled the pinto round and it was the grey's turn to toss her head and act a little temperamental. She'd been with Hart so long she didn't take to close company from some other horse.

Tap Loughlin had moved back to the door; he was resting the underside of one boot against it, watching as Hart drew away, heading for the wide blue of the lake and then the road to the border. As Tap watched him go he thought about the speed with which the Colt had appeared in Hart's hand and prayed that Majors would see it too, only that it wouldn't end there.

He prayed that one of the bullets Hart was carrying had Lloyd Majors' name writ deep into its casing.

Thirteen

Scott Levy was sweating so much he could smell himself even through the stink of horse sweat that surrounded him. The flies were paying as much attention to him as they were to his mount. The leather of the reins slipped between his fingers as he pushed the animal into a canter and then slowed it again to a trot. There were trees in both sides of the trail now, scrub scrambling away from them and merging with the tall grass. Here and there small-headed flowers showed yellow or blue through the pervading green.

The gunshot wound he'd taken in his thigh was reminding him of its presence.

His pistol felt heavy and unwieldy at his side.

The blue-green of his eyes shone back the sun more startled than ever.

'Hold it!'

Levy stuttered forward in the saddle at the command, hauling on the rein so hard that the horse whinnied and reared.

'It's me!' Levy shouted. 'Me, Scott!'

'Hold it there!'

Levy clamped his knees tight against the horse's sides and waited as the man appeared from the trees to the right of the track. He was further back than Levy had thought from the fall of his voice and it was a few moments before he recognized him for certain as Bluey – tall and rangey, a shock of fair hair forever threatening to fall right over his eyes and blind him. He couldn't have been much over seventeen.

'That really you, Scott?'

Levy laughed nervously; broke off quickly, recognizing the strangeness of the sound. 'Sure it's me. Who d'you think it is?'

'Don't rightly . . . Jesus, Scotty, it's good to see a friendly face!'

Levy laughed again, a little more easily this time. He reached down his hand and the youngster clasped it tight, not noticing the fact that it was running with sweat.

'Where the . . . how come you're here? We thought you was clapped up in the State Pen.'

'We was.'

'And?'

Levy almost giggled. 'We bust out.'

'How many of you?'

'Whole damned lot of us, no less.'

Bluey shook his head and the hair toppled down on to his forehead, pieces touching the bridge of his nose; he slapped his leg and shrilly whistled. 'Tap an' the whole bunch?'

'Tap an' me, Baptiste and Little Kinney.'

Bluey almost hugged himself with excitement. 'Well, where are they?'

Levy nodded back down the trail. 'They'll be along. Sent me on ahead to see if you was cooped up here. That's what.' He looked at Bluey and smiled.

Bluey ran his fingers up through his hair and shook his head from one side to the other, the hair falling down again and making question marks over his face. 'That Tap,' he sang out, excited. 'I knew he'd think of somethin'. Knew he wasn't dumb enough to let them bastards swing him from no gallows. Hey! That Tap – he sure is some feller, ain't he? Ain't he, Scott?'

Levy agreed, a knot of discomfort tightening at the base of his stomach. 'Let's ride up, shall we, Bluey?'

'Yeah, sure, we . . . but the road, Scott. Jeff says we got to guard the road in case some posse . . .'

Levy treated him to his best reassuring smile. 'Hold on to yourself, now, Bluey. Remember Tap and the rest of the boys is back there. They'll give this piece of track all the guardin' it needs.'

'Hah!' Bluey slapped his leg and tickled his own ribs and his face shone like a ten-year-old's come Christmas. 'You're right, Scott. No need to guard the road with Tap comin' on up it.' He beamed. 'What signal you got arranged with him.'

'Simple. Any trouble, I fire twice, then once. They don't hear nothin', it's okay to come through.'

Bluey shook his head, delighted by the simplicity of it all.

'Let's get up an' see Jeff, eh?'

'Sure, Scott. Can't wait till I see his face.'

Jeff's face was partly covered by a reddish half-formed beard that Levy hadn't seen before. He was sitting out back of the cabin, peeling potatoes into an oaken bucket and thinking about the times his ma had sat by their farm in Virginia, doing the self-same thing. When he heard the horse approaching, he dropped the potato in the water and by the time the rippling had subsided, his Winchester was to his shoulder and a shell had been levered into the chamber.

'Okay, Jeff!' hollered Bluey. 'It's Scott! An' the rest of the bunch are comin' on behind.'

Jeff didn't lower the rifle till he could see the two colours of Levy's eyes clear and distinct. Then he let his face crack into a smile, the smile became a laugh, the laugh almost tears. The small, hunched figure of Scott Levy getting down from the saddle and limping over towards him was the best thing he'd seen in a coon's age.

'How far behind?' asked Jeff, pointing down towards the path through the trees.

'Mile or so, maybe,' said Levy.

'Let's go meet 'em.'

'No, better get inside and hustle up some food an' coffee. Long time since Tap and the rest got a good meal inside 'em.'

'Okay!' agreed Jeff, clapping Levy on his humped back. 'Let's get in an' do that. Kind of a surprise for 'em, huh?'

'Yeah,' said Levy, 'a surprise.'

Levy dragged an empty barrel over towards the bunks along the right-hand wall, close to the front end. He shucked off his coat, but he was careful to keep his gun belt buckled on. He noticed that Jeff had set his rifle down to the left of the door and had only a knife in a sheath on his belt. Bluey had rested his rifle next to Jeff's and was toting a pistol, holstered at his side.

The two men hurried around, preparing the welcome meal, telling Levy he should rest. He leaned back against the front wall and asked them about their escape from the posse and about the money.

'Tap don't have to worry 'bout that,' said Bluey. 'Does he, Jeff?'

'We got it safe,' said Jeff. 'Buried it safe under the boards here.'

'All of it?' asked Levy, perhaps a fraction too anxiously.

'Most.'

'Most?'

'You'll never guess what we did,' said Jeff, rubbing his hands down the front of his plaid shirt. 'Tap goin' to be real pleased when he hears.'

'Go on,' said Levy.

'We took six hundred dollars up to that schoolteacher.'

'Yeah,' said Bluey. 'That one in Springfield he was sparkin'.'

Levy stood up. 'What the hell you do that for?'

The two men looked at one another, surprised by the change of tone in Levy's voice.

'Figured he'd want it that way,' said Jeff.

'We didn't know what was goin' to happen to him down in the State Pen,' said Bluey. 'She's holdin' on to it for him. Said she wasn't goin' to spend a nickel. Not till she . . . till she knew for sure what happened to Tap.'

'Still . . .' Levy began.

Bluey gestured with his hands outwards. 'Come on, Scott, it don't matter none. There's more'n enough left for the rest of us. You know that.'

Levy shrugged and sat back down. 'Yeah. I reckon you're right.'

'An' you do think Tap'll be pleased, don't you?' asked Bluey a little anxiously.

'Yeah,' said Levy. 'I think Tap'll be pleased and then some.'

Bluey and Jeff looked at one another and nodded, smiles on both their faces. Levy leaned back against the wall and the others got back to their chores. They were still fussing round the stove when the cabin door was hurled back and three men burst into the space.

'Hey!' Jeff whirled fast and saw a man bulking inside the doorway with a gun held out in front of him. He didn't know who he was, but sure as hell knew it wasn't Tap Loughlin. Jeff swung his arm and hurled pan and contents towards the big man's face, throwing himself to the far side of the stove as he did so.

Majors didn't even bother to duck; he let the pan strike his chest and bounce away; he angled his pistol round and squinted along the top of the barrel. He fired three times. Jeff was driven back against the stove, his legs hitting it hard, a pot of coffee falling down, the contents spilling over Jeff's face and arm. The coffee was hot and black and it scalded the open skin, but already Jeff wasn't worrying. The three slugs had torn their way through chest and neck and before Jeff's bearded face struck the boards he was about as dead as he was going to be.

Across from him, Bluey leaned his body forward, hand to the butt of his holstered gun. His mouth was open, tongue protruding between open lips. His hair hung down almost shielding his eyes but not enough – he could still see what had happened. He was shaking, shaking like a small kid afraid for the first time. A small kid that comes face to face with the bogieman.

Bluey looked at Majors and the two blacks at back of him. He looked at them and slapped his left thigh; he laughed and pulled at his gun. Joseph tighted the butt of the sawn-off shotgun against his hip and squeezed down on both triggers.

Smiling, Bluey's guts were spread all over the cabin.

Levy was sitting in the corner on top of the barrel, his pistol drawn but unused.

Majors hollered his appreciation for what Joseph had done, flicked a few sprays of blood and tissue away from his clothes and asked Levy if they'd told him where the money was.

'Sure,' said Levy, and told Majors what they'd said.

Majors nodded, turned, turned back and shot Levy through the side of the head.

The blue and green eyes looked startled even as he died.

'What you . . . ?' Gideon began asking, till a quick glance from Joseph warned him to hold his tongue.

Majors answered him anyway. 'He was one of Loughlin's bunch. No way you could ever trust him. Besides, all that money goes a lot further split three ways, don't it?'

'Sure,' agreed Joseph slowly. 'Close to two thousand dollars each.'

Majors shook his head. 'Let's think on that. I'm runnin' this show, ain't I? I get more of the cut. That's the way it has to be.'

Gideon and Joseph looked at one another, at the dead men spread across the room, back at Majors again. 'All right,' Joseph said, 'it seems fair to us.'

'Yeah. Half for me, the rest split between the two of you. And that's the way we'll run things from here on in.'

The two blacks said nothing; neither of them wanted to cross Majors there and then. Even half divided between them was more money than they'd ever reckoned to see in a lifetime down in Bogalusa. And if they stuck with the big man a while longer, there might be even more. Majors had been sounding off about how taking banks was easy and if a weak fool like Tap Loughlin had made a good living at it, then they were sure to do better.

Majors dipped his fingers into what food remained inside the pan Jeff had thrown against his chest. He ate it hungrily and licked his finger ends clean.

'We'd best get to diggin' up this money, boys,' he said, making it clear that what he meant was that they had best get to doing it.

There was a long-handled shovel racked against the far corner of the cabin and Gideon soon found a claw-hammer amongst a box of rusting tools. They set their muscles to work and Majors picked at the remnants of the food and watched. As soon as the boards had been lifted and the earth was beginning to be thrown back, he joined in, spelling the two blacks, his greed getting the better of his idleness.

The money had been buried in the sacks Tap's men had taken it away in, those sacks set into an old packing case with warped, loose sides. Gideon was digging when the case was struck by the shovel blade and his smile rang true through the sweat that ran liberally down his face.

In only a few minutes, all three men were sitting on a heap of old floorboards, staring at five and a half thousand dollars.

'When we've counted this,' said Majors, 'we'll share it out. Right off.'

'Yeah,' agreed Gideon and Joseph together.

'Then we'll ride on out of this stinkin' hole.'

'Yeah.'

'North.'

Gideon and Joseph looked at him for an explanation.

'We've got us six hundred more dollars owin'. I intend to see we collect.'

From Shadow Point to Springfield was a good day's ride and the three men had to break their journey somewhere. Rossiter seemed as good a place as any. No more than a dozen buildings clustered around a well and a windmill, it squatted in the middle of the plain like something that had long since been forgotten. One general store, one livery stable, one saloon. That represented the sum total of Rossiter's commercial enterprise. The dogs swapped fleas around all summer and spent most of the winter forgetting where they'd hidden their bones.

Majors and the two blacks tied up the horses to the corral post to the side of the livery stable, while Majors went in to trade.

'All right,' he said a few minutes later. 'We can get the mounts fed and watered. There's a hay barn we can throw down in for the night. That's about the best this one-eyed place does for a hotel. Gideon, you take these horses inside, meet us over at the saloon.'

Inside the Rossiter Empress, the same card game was going on that seemed to have been going on for the past five years. The bartender reluctantly set down his hand and shuffled to the bar in broken-backed shoes. He didn't want to disturb a winning run to serve anyone, let alone a nigger. Would have said so, too, except for him being big and armed and having a white feller with him who was even bigger if anything.

He wiped at his runny nose with the side of his hand and asked what they wanted. He was wiping the dust from the whisky bottle when a second nigger walked in, looking just like the first. He almost dropped the bottle there and then.

Old Ed, dealing a fresh hand, set down three cards on the same spot before realizing what he was doing.

Majors dropped a coin on to the counter and snatched the bottle away. Joseph carried three stained and chipped glasses. There were tables enough to choose from and Majors picked one close to the back of the room, where he could sit and face the door.

The three men sat for a while, drinking in silence, letting the whisky get to their veins. Occasionally one or other of the card players would turn his head and glance round to see what the strangers were doing, but after fifteen minutes or so, the cards became more important.

Majors was drinking fast and starting to brag about what they'd done and what they were going to do in the future. The light slowly started to fade inside the room and the bartender got up to light a pair of kerosene lamps, one more or less directly above the card table, the other over the bar. Two circles of light, shifting a little in the wind that cut above the door, spilled over the edge of the table at which the three men sat.

'Why the hell ain't there no women in this place?'

Gideon and Joseph tried to reason with Majors, quieten him down.

'I said,' Majors shouted, pushing away Joseph's restraining hand, 'why the hell ain't there no women? What kind of a saloon is this without women in it?' Majors stood up too quickly, knocking the table sideways, sending a couple of the glasses to the floor with a crash.

Gideon caught the bottle before it fell too, though there was little enough left inside.

'You! You!' Majors was pointing at the bartender, who was busy looking at his cards and pretending not to notice. 'Where are all the whores around here?'

Old Ed Davison chuckled to himself and said: 'You think if we knew the answer to that one we'd be sittin' here playin' poker?'

But Majors didn't hear what Ed had said, only knew that he'd said something. He started out towards him and Joseph stood up and intercepted him. Majors saw the black in his path and tried to brush him aside. It wasn't that easy.

'Let's sit back down,' said Joseph forcefully.

'I'll do what I damn well please!'

'Sure. Only why don't we finish this bottle an' then we can all go whorin' when we're done. There's got to be women somewhere, ain't there?'

Majors ground his teeth together and went to go past Joseph again, but still the big Negro blocked his path, standing square in front of him, one hand restraining Majors' right arm.

'C'mon,' called Gideon from the table. 'Sooner we get rid of this bottle, sooner we can buy another. Ain't that so, Joseph?'

'Sure,' replied Joseph. 'Sure, that's right. Let's get it done.'

He succeeded in turning Majors round and shifting him back to his seat. Gideon recovered the glasses from the floor and set them down.

'C'mon,' he said. 'Let's have a drink.'

Majors swayed a little and his breath came heavily; his face lurched towards Joseph's and the thought flashed through the Negro's mind that maybe now was the time to make a break. Hit Majors but good when he wasn't expecting it and leave him cold. Grab the horses, take their share of the money and ride anywhere but where Majors was heading. What did another five hundred dollars matter when you had as much as was already waiting to be spent?

But Majors grasped Joseph hard on the upper arm and nodded his head. 'You're right. You're both right. Let's get another bottle.'

He pulled a greenback from his pants pocket with a mixture of speed and dexterity that made Joseph glad he hadn't put his thoughts into action. Majors was nowhere near as drunk as he was letting on.

'You get it. Huh?'

Joseph didn't think much to running errands, but he took the bill anyway and went over to the bar. The bartender glanced over his shoulder and called to hang on a minute – he had a good enough hand not to want to throw it in on account of one bottle of whisky. Joseph leaned back against the counter and hooked his boot heel over the wooden rail that ran close to the floor.

Majors and Gideon were finishing what remained of the first bottle and the big man seemed to have calmed down. He was sitting with one arm spread wide across the table, the other angled towards his mouth. Joseph stared at Majors, his thoughts about him torn between admiration for his strength and resolution and contempt for his sheer callousness, his apparent lack of self-control. If there was one thing a black learned down low on the Mississippi, it was self-control.

Over at the table, the bartender cursed as his three eights weren't good enough. Scraping back his chair, he stood up and began to turn. He didn't get more than halfway round – he stopped short and stared at the doorway.

Hart had come up soft. He'd tied his own mounts lower down the short street; checked with the man at the livery stable that the horses of the three strangers were all tied up safe, unsaddled and far from ready for a quick getaway. Then he walked slow and easy back down to the saloon. It was a single door and it pushed back with scarcely a squeak. Hart had his hat angled down towards the right, the striped Indian blanket was draped over his left shoulder, left arm and hip. Underneath the blanket he was wearing a faded red shirt, ringed with different shades of sweat. His pants were brown and worn over scuffed brown boots of a darker shade. The pearl-handled Colt Peacemaker sat snug in its holster and the small leather thong which fitted over the hammer had been slipped free. A second length of leather, attached to the bottom of the holster, was tied tight inside his thigh.

Hart stood one pace inside the doorway and allowed the heavy wooden door to swing slowly, almost silently, shut behind him.

One of the card players began coughing, raw and harsh, and couldn't find a way to stop. Another, without knowing it, drummed his finger ends to an irregular pattern underneath the table top. The bartender, mouth slightly open, stood almost erect and stared.

Joseph had followed the barman's look and as soon as he saw the figure in the doorway, his hand started to move towards his gun.

'Don't!'

Joseph's hand froze.

At the back of the room, Majors lurched awkwardly to his feet, pushing the table hard into Gideon's chest and dislodging one of the glasses. It fell to the ground without breaking and started to roll in a decreasing number of arcs, the rim rattling on the uneven edges of the boards.

'Majors!' called Hart.

The big man swayed a little and watching him from the corner of his eye, Joseph was certain he was exaggerating again. Trying to gain himself an edge.

'Lloyd Majors?'

'Who the hell wants to know?'

Majors squared himself round and jutted his head belligerently forward. His gun arm began to arch out from his body and his feet shifted themselves inches further apart, adjusting the balance.

Two of the card players shifted their chairs away from the table and scuttled towards the side wall. The one who was coughing sat doubled over, his nose almost resting on a hand of cards, his whole body racked. Above him, the bartender still hadn't moved; his eyes still hadn't left Hart's face.

Joseph was continuing to look at the pearl-handled Colt, then at the blanket, wondering.

'You men there,' said Hart, nodding at the card table, 'get clear.'

The order jerked the bartender into movement; he helped the coughing man towards the side, the continuous rasping sound cutting through the saloon like a saw jammed into a knot of wood.

'Majors,' said Hart, 'I'm takin' you back. You two . . .' His eyes shifted quickly from Gideon to Joseph and back again. '. . . I ain't interested in. Keep out of this an' where you go ain't my concern.'

Joseph heard the words but stuck at believing them. What kind of a lawman was this? What kind of bounty hunter? Didn't he know how much they were carrying?

Hart read the Negro's thoughts.

'I'm not with the railroad,' he said. 'Not the law. I don't care about what you dug up at Shadow Point. I just want him.'

And Hart's words pointed directly at Lloyd Majors and no one else.

Majors angled his arm a little more steeply. 'You want me,' he called down the room, 'you're goin' to have to take the three of us.'

Hart nodded: 'If that's the way it's got to be. Only I wouldn't be so certain I was callin' all the shots.'

Majors turned his head fractionally and glared at Gideon; he nodded, bull-like, at Joseph midway along the bar. 'Three of us,' he repeated.

'Maybe.'

Gideon's mind was racing, jumbled. His thoughts broke between the sawn-off shotgun that was resting between the folded saddle bags on the floor, less than a couple of feet away from his right boot, and the length of the room between where he was standing and the door. If he and Joseph could get clear and ride . . .

Sweat broke from his temples: he knew for certain that the moment he made that kind of a move, Majors would shoot him in the back.

'I'll take that gun, Majors.' Hart still hadn't moved, he could see the entire saloon from where he was, covering everyone as they stood in and out of the circles of light that pooled down from the pair of lamps.

'Now. Use your left hand and ease it out.'

'Go to hell!'

Hart shook his head. 'Uh-uh. That's where you'll go the minute you call the wrong move.'

Joseph unhooked his boot from the rail. 'Who are you, mister?' he asked.

'Majors, he stabbed a youngster to death, raped a girl. Their old man don't think he should be runnin' free after doin' that.'

'You're takin' me back to prison?' demanded Majors, loud-voiced.

Hart shook his head again. 'I'm takin' you back to those kids' old man.' The first traces of a smile appeared around the edges of Hart's mouth. 'He says he's goin' to string you up with his own hands. An' I think I just might help him do it.'

Majors threw back his head suddenly and laughed – a rough, roaring sound that grated the air. He flung out his left arm wide and at the same time his right hand dived, fingers clutching, towards the gun at his hip.

Hart's own hand blurred through a fast curve and climbed.

Majors' laugh choked to a spluttering silence as he felt the hardness of the pistol butt slap against his palm and his fingers tightened on wood and metal.

His massive body dipped further as he dragged the pistol up. The front sight snagged against the holster as Hart levelled his Colt and allowed himself time to aim. In a fractured second Majors saw him, saw the gun, continued to draw. Hart shot him through the left side, splintering two ribs over the heart. The big man's arm was still lifting, rising; his fingers were opening, clutching blindly for the pistol grip as it slid away.

Majors stumbled three, four paces back and then heaved himself to the side, sending the table crashing to the ground as he slumped over it. He moaned and lifted his head, slamming it back down on the edge of the fallen table as if somehow that would obliterate the pain that was tearing jaggedly through him.

Gideon backed off, lifting his own hands level with his head, not wanting the stranger to think he was about to interfere. At the bar, Joseph still hadn't made up his mind, still couldn't believe that this man was about to let them ride free.

Majors slammed his head a second time, breaking the skin. He snarled and fell, only he wasn't falling, he was diving for the shotgun on the ground.

Hart thumbed back the hammer and waited until Majors began to straighten. Then he fired twice, the shots so close together that their sound merged into one explosion. The slugs tore away a fist-sized hole at the point where the breast bone had been before the impact splintered it away. One bullet lodged up against the collar bone, the other burst through Majors' back taking with it a welter of ruptured tissue and bloodied bone.

'Jesus Christ!' Joseph started forward, hesitated, hung his right hand over his pistol butt.

Hart shook the blanket free of his left arm and revealed the ten-gauge Remington, its fourteen-inch barrels pointing straight at Joseph and ready to blow him away.

The black rocked on his heels and caught his breath: slow and deliberate, he spread both arms wide, wide as they could go.

Majors finished falling. The length of his body crashed against the boards and the sound echoed dully up and down the saloon. One heel hammered a brief tattoo on the boards and it was done. Except that the blood continued to pump from the four holes in his body. Except that the sphincter muscle loosened and the room was suddenly filled with the stink of human rot.

The bartender hurried across the room and jerked open a bottle, tilting it back and drinking hard. Two of the others half-ran, half-shuffled for the door and Hart stepped aside to let them through. The two blacks were still waiting, hands surrendering.

'We got no quarrel?' Hart asked, looking from one to the other.

Neither man spoke or moved.

'You ain't fixin' to do somethin' 'bout that?' He looked at Majors stretched out along the floor.

'Uh-uh,' gulped Gideon.

'No, sir.' Joseph shook his head and let his arms fall back to his sides. 'You don't want nothin' more from us, we got no words to have with you.'

'Okay.' Hart moved a couple of paces deeper into the room. 'One thing you can do before you ride out. There's a couple of horses out front. Take him out and wrap him in the blanket tied across the pinto. Rope him over the saddle. I'm taking him back.'

Gideon and Joseph looked at one another and shrugged. Then Joseph went outside to get the blanket, Gideon used his boot to turn Majors slowly over on to his back.

Hart stepped across to the bar and ordered a whisky: he figured he'd earned it.

Fourteen

The ride back down to the Arkansas border was made quickly enough, but from there to Cass it was nothing more than a drag, a slow penance for some sin Hart remained ignorant of yet was being forced to atone for. Midway between Garfield and his destination Hart crossed tracks with the Hardcastle wagon. He was sure to tether the pinto and its burden some distance off before riding across on the grey and saying hello, passing the time of day. Hardcastle himself looked as battered and care-worn as his top hat and Hart would have suggested a double dose of cure-all had he imagined that it would have done any good. Whatever benefit it had been to Loughlin's men had worn off soon enough at the end of the Pinkertons' guns.

'You got what you was lookin' for then?' said Myra from the depths of her fur coat. The baby was asleep in her lap, thumb in mouth.

Hart said nothing, nodded.

'That feller who I was talkin' with while his friends were getting patched up – that ain't him?'

'No.'

'You run into him, though?'

Hardcastle swished at a couple of flies playing tag in front of his face and tried not to get edgy about the wistfulness that was creeping into Myra's voice.

'Yeah,' answered Hart. 'I saw him.'

'He survived the meeting?' asked Myra, sarcasm giving the question a cutting tone that made Hardcastle grind the heel of his boot hard into the boards.

'He survived,' said Hart. 'Rode north far as I know. Springfield way. Something about a woman up there.'

Myra twisted up the right side of her mouth and shifted her shoulders beneath her coat. Hardcastle only prevented himself from smiling – a gesture he figured might bring him trouble – by starting to whistle through his teeth.

'Be seein' you folk,' said Hart, touching his hat and wheeling the grey away from the wagon.

Hardcastle raised his hand in a salute; Myra glanced at him once and then began fussing the baby. Before Hart had regained the pinto, the child's cries were clearly heard.

Tap Loughlin had indeed headed for Springfield. On two occasions he'd almost run into trouble: once he narrowly avoided riding smack into a posse combing the country for a bunch of cattle rustlers; another time he rode into a small trading post no more than half an hour after a couple of straight-faced Pinkerton men had been in there asking questions about a couple of outlaw blacks.

Tap bought some food and ammunition and lit out quick, making sure he didn't follow in the same direction the detectives had taken. He was pretty shaken up by coming that close to them, but not displeased at what he'd heard. If they were running down Gideon and Joseph that meant it was likely the feller he talked with at Cooper's Stand had lived up to his word and seen that Majors wasn't running loose. It also likely meant that the railroad money wasn't stashed away at Shadow Point any more – if it was, then no Pinks were going to be wasting their time chasing after a couple of niggers. No – he was steering clear of the old hide-out. It was Springfield and Sara-Lee and the sooner he got there – without taking any unnecessary risks – the better.

Tap eventually reached Springfield on a Sunday night, long

after the bell for services had sounded and been forgotten. After those folk who had gone to listen to the Word had changed back out of their go-to-meeting clothes and the preacher's words were faded and past.

There was no light showing through the windows of the small single-storey house where Sara-Lee lived, and Tap hesitated, surprised. She might have gone calling on friends, but by that time of night . . .

He tied up the horse and walked around back. No light: no sound. Back at the front he tried the front door and it gave to his touch. Swung back with a grating sound as the underside rubbed over the floor. Tap felt the hairs at the back of his neck prickle and he drew the pistol from his belt. He waited. Listening, he cocked the hammer and the click was like the snapping of dry twigs underfoot.

Tap stepped inside.

Nothing moved. He stood inside the doorway, allowing his eyes to become accustomed to the light. Gradually, Sara's armchair emerged from the gloom, the small table, round and polished, at which she wrote. Tap imagined he could smell the lavender from the small vase of dried herbs which stood at its centre. He saw the dresser, with its cups and plates neatly displayed; the straight-backed chairs. The fireplace was bare and the rug in front of it where he and Sara had first . . .

Tap closed the door behind him and took a match from his pocket. The lamp stuttered to life. The only shadows moving inside the room were Tap's own. He went into the bedroom, the pantry, the outhouse. None of the furniture had been moved, nothing of substance had vanished. But of anything personal to Sara there was no trace. No clothing; no pictures remained hanging from the walls; the bookshelves she had made from stray planks of wood and packing cases now held only a few unused sheets of paper and a quantity of dust. The leather-bound volume of Shakespearean plays that had been her most treasured possession no longer held pride of place in a section of its own.

Tap's head swam. He went, not quite steadily, to the armchair and sat down. He knew there had to be a good reason, a sensible explanation – all he needed to do was sit for a while and figure it out.

Bright sunlight fell across the clearing, sending sharp, knife-edged shadows across the house. The walls gleamed yellow and white.

Despite the warmth of the day, smoke nevertheless drifted skywards from one of the chimneys. Hart unfastened the low gate and remounted, leading his grisly burden towards the flight of steps and the high brick archway. Before he came to a halt, the door had opened and Grant stepped out. He was wearing a dark suit, the jacket unbuttoned, his shirt loose at the neck and tieless. His eyes were unnaturally bright within the fleshy spread of his face.

'That's him?' A pink edge of tongue showed between his lips and his fleshy hands toyed with the lapels of his suit.

Hart nodded, dismounted. The body was stiff as boards hammered carelessly together but it stank like nothing imaginable.

Grant descended the steps quickly, his excitement clear. He grasped the reins of the pinto and hauled on them hard so that the animal tried to twist away.

'You're sure it's Majors?' Grant's fingers were at the end of the blanket. The material had dried to the body, glued fast with congealed blood. Hart didn't know what the banker intended to do or how; he didn't care. All he wanted was to get his payment and leave. Ride as far away from there as he could and fast. He wanted to put some distance between the Grant place and himself and then soak himself in water that was hot enough to scald the pervading stench away from his skin. Away from his mind.

'You're not gettin' down,' said Grant.

'That's right.'

'I don't understand.'

'That don't matter. Just bring me what we reckoned an' I'll leave.'

'Now? You stay. We've got somethin' to celebrate. This miserable bastard took my son and daughter both – don't you forget it!'

Hart wasn't about to forget: not any of it. 'The money,' he said.

Grant looked at him and saw from the set of the lean, leathered face that Hart wasn't about to change his mind.

'All right.' The banker went back up the steps and into the house. In less than five minutes he returned with a small cotton bag. Hart reached down and took it from him, stuffed it immediately into one of his saddle bags.

'Surely you're going to count it?'

Hart didn't answer. He didn't nod his head or touch the brim of his hat. He turned the grey away and as he did so he saw what he had not wanted to see: the silhouette of the girl against the far window, held there by the brightness of the sun. The image clung to Hart's mind as he sought the trail south – the girl and what he had brought back to her.

Tap had fallen asleep in the armchair and not woken until well past dawn. Nothing in the room had changed. He sat there for a long time, his mind uncertain and unfocused. Then he went into town and began asking questions. He went to the general store, to the school; he asked anyone he imagined might have some idea where Sara-Lee had gone. No one knew: no one had heard her say a goodbye or a farewell. She had said nothing to the other teacher at the school, she had bought no supplies from the store that suggested a journey. No ticket had been booked in her name at the stage line. There was nothing to give Tap the slightest clue until he went to the railroad station and spoke with the clerk.

The clerk was a bald, bumbling man who was deaf in one ear and could pretend to be deaf in his good ear too if it suited him. He was quite deaf to Tap's questions until some money appeared on the table between them. Then he remembered – or thought he did – that a woman who might have been Sara-Lee had bought a ticket east. No, he didn't think it was St Louis – Chicago sounded more like. Even more money couldn't make the clerk more definite than that. After all, it had been weeks ago and with all the folk who used the railroad . . .

So she had caught the Aitchison, Topeka and Santa Fe. The same train she had persuaded him he ought to hold up. Big money, real money, she had said: then we can go away together. Leave this place behind us.

She hadn't waited for him.

On his way back to the house that evening, his mind fuzzy with drink from an afternoon's morose session in the saloon, a head came out through the window of the place close alongside. A woman who remembered Sara-Lee having a couple of visitors, men who'd ridden up early one morning. They hadn't stayed long, the woman assured Tap. It was as if they'd been delivering something. She had no idea what. But after that day, she didn't see Sara-Lee again.

Tap asked the woman if she could recall what either of the callers had looked like.

At first she didn't think she could, but then she remembered that one of them – the younger one – had a lot of fair hair that fell down across his face as if it might go in his eyes. She recalled that clear as if he was standing there now.

'I don't know what they could have brought that made Sara-Lee leave so sudden,' said the neighbour. She smiled hesitantly at Tap and then went back to her own affairs.

Tap went inside the house and closed the door with a slam behind him: he could guess what Bluey and Jeff had brought – they had brought Sara-Lee his share of the money. She had got her train money after all.

Tap pulled a half-bottle of whisky from his pocket and took a long swallow. He shut the blinds against the outside and sat deep in the armchair. He knew nothing about the other questions that were being asked in Springfield that afternoon by two grim-faced men whose interests very much coincided with his own. He was sitting greyly in the chair with the bottle tilted in his hand and the memory of Sara nagging at his brain when they approached the house.

Charlie Deuce and his partner had caught up with the two blacks sleeping rough close to the Kansas border. They had got close enough to be able to shoot them where they lay, a bullet apiece in the head and neither Gideon nor Joseph had woken up.

Now they stepped carefully up to the Danziger house, Deuce to the front door and Carey towards the back.

The sound of the back door opening spun Tap round.

'Sara!' he called . . .

Wes Hart sat back in the enamel bath tub and scrubbed at his body. A chair stood close to the right side of the tub and his gun belt hung over it, the butt of the Colt within easy reach. He wasn't about to risk any more visits from Marshal Fagan nor anyone else who might want to get the drop on him, send him off on a job of work. The money he'd got from Grant was in his pants pocket: the image of the silent, unmoving girl was still imprinted on the back of his mind.

There was no way of Hart knowing, but were he able to return to the house outside Cass, the picture he would see would be slightly different. Katherine Grant's silhouette still clung close to the window of her room, only now it was not quite still. Rather, it swayed with the movement of the rope, her feet tapping against the glass. Again, again, again.

Her father had got his hanging, though not as he had imagined, not with his own hands.

Selected Bestsellers

☐	**Extraterrestrial Civilizations**	Isaac Asimov	£1.50p
☐	**Pregnancy**	Gordon Bourne	£2.75p
☐	**Options**	Freda Bright	£1.50p
☐	**The Thirty-nine Steps**	John Buchan	80p
☐	**Out of Practice**	Rob Buckman	95p
☐	**The Flowers of the Forest**	Elizabeth Byrd	£1.50p
☐	**The 35mm Photographer's Handbook**	Julian Calder and John Garrett	£5.95p
☐	**Secret of Blackoaks**	Ashley Carter	£1.50p
☐	**A Night of Gaiety**	Barbara Cartland	90p
☐	**The Sittaford Mystery**	Agatha Christie	£1.00p
☐	**Lovers and Gamblers**	Jackie Collins	£1.95p
☐	**Sphinx**	Robin Cook	£1.25p
☐	**Soft Furnishings**	Designers' Guild	£5.95p
☐	**Rebecca**	Daphne du Maurier	£1.50p
☐	**Travellers' France**	Arthur Eperon	£2.50p
☐	**Travellers' Italy**	Arthur Eperon	£2.50p
☐	**The Complete Calorie Counter**	Eileen Fowler	50p
☐	**The Diary of Anne Frank**	Anne Frank	95p
☐	**Blitz**	David Fraser	£1.95p
☐	**Flashman**	George MacDonald Fraser	£1.25p
☐	**Linda Goodman's Sun Signs**	Linda Goodman	£1.95p
☐	**The 38th Pan Book of Crosswords**	Mike Grimshaw	80p
☐	**The Moneychangers**	Arthur Hailey	£1.95p
☐	**Secrets**	Unity Hall	£1.50p
☐	**The Maltese Falcon**	Dashiell Hammett	95p
☐	**Vets Might Fly**	James Herriot	£1.25p
☐	**Simon the Coldheart**	Georgette Heyer	95p
☐	**The Eagle Has Landed**	Jack Higgins	£1.50p
☐	**Mountbatten: Hero of Our Time**	Richard Hough	£1.95p
☐	**The Marchand Woman**	John Ives	£1.25p
☐	**Smiley's People**	John le Carré	£1.75p
☐	**To Kill a Mockingbird**	Harper Lee	£1.25p
☐	**How to be a Gifted Parent**	David Lewis	£1.95p
☐	**The Empty Hours**	Ed McBain	£1.25p
☐	**Shanghai**	William Marshall	£1.25p

John B. Harvey

Hart 8: John Wesley Hardin 85p

In the old West, gunfighting was a trade you started early. Wes Hart killed his first man when he was still in his teens, and so did John Wesley Hardin. Hardin went on to carve himself a notch in the history books as an outlaw with all the virtue of a renegade rattlesnake. A posse of Rangers had marked Wes Hardin down for the reckoning. Riding with them was Wes Hart, the Regulator . . .

William Wingate

Hardacre £1.50

He came to the town of Baptist's Fire with a job to do. It was a town in the fist of a boss man with enough hired muscle to handle anything – anything but Hardacre . . .

'Drawling humour, way-out sex, violence in buckets . . . a book you'll remember' THE TIMES

'There is a power – a raw strength – in Wingate's writing that is unquestionably original . . . a disturbing and memorable book' DAILY TELEGRAPH

James Albany

SAS 1: Warrior's Caste 95p

Book 1 in the fighting saga of the SAS. France 1940 – as the Panzers pursued their thrust to the sea, a crack SS unit came to the small town of St Felice, in search of a very special English fugitive. Their orders from the Führer were to take the Englishman whatever the cost. But other men were coming to St Felice – Lieutenant Deacon and the burly Canadian Buz Campbell, with a secret weapon that the SS couldn't match: Corporal McNair. Their job – to find the mysterious Englishman and bring him back alive.

John B. Harvey

Hart 1: Cherokee Outlet 85p

Wes Hart is *The Regulator*. Ex-soldier, ex-Texas Ranger, ex-rider with Billy the Kid, he's tough, ruthless and slick with a .45. He's for hire now and he isn't cheap. When a double-crossing gunman called Quint stole Hart's horse from a Stillwater saloon Hart went all out to see his blood spattered all over the Eufaula prairie. Then Quint joined a cattle-rustling set-up under Belle Starr, and Hart was appointed to clean them up real good.

Hart 2: Blood Trail 85p

The trickle of blood from a scalped corpse in a deathly quiet Stillwater saloon told Hart that the Cheyenne had paid a visit . . . but there had to be a reason. A crooked rancher called Fredericks is engaged in a shady deal with the Cheyenne, Belle Starr is involved too, and it's up to Hart to sort things out.

Hart 5: Blood on the Border 85p

The good citizens of Caldwell had raised a fistful of dollars to pay for the railroad that would bring the Santa Fe thundering to their town. It was not a popular idea with Shire, the local cattle baron. Then the money was carried off by three of the nastiest desperados the border country had seen. Which explains how the townsfolk are paying out to Wes Hart the Regulator. For Hart it's another job, but one with a pretty widow woman as well as a payday . . .

Hart 6: Ride the Wide Country 85p

The train had a special load aboard. The Regulator's lady and her two young kids. Then the desperados came. He'd fought them before, back in Caldwell. After a red-hot hailstorm of lead, one of the victims was one of those kids. Hart knew those killers had to pay in blood, and he was going to do the debt-collecting – with a little help from Rose, a lady of the night with her own reasons to get even . . .